THE GAME OF ZYPHORA

KEERTHANA RAMKUMAR

Contents

Preface   v

HOOK   vii

About the Author   ix

1. The Lens Of Unseen Realms   1

2. The Silent Secret   7

3. The Whispers Of The Dark   13

4. The Call Of The Game   17

5. Ammama's Warning   25

6. The Dark Invitation   31

7. The Pause Before The Storm   37

8. The Mysterious Room   47

9. The Silent Game   51

10. The Horse And The Knight   55

11. The Dark Path Ahead   59

12. The Red Prison   65

13. The Flame Of Despair   69

14. The Dice Of Fate   75

15. Falling Into The Game   79

16. The Queen's Entry   83

17. The Ticking Clock   87

18. The Silent Queen   93

19. The Game's Edge   97

20. The King's Command   105

21. The Game Unfolds   117

Contents

22. Turning Point   125

23. The Final Move   129

24. The Crown's Awakening   135

Preface

The Game of Zyphora is the result of an idea that's been with me for as long as I can remember. A thought that has evolved into a story full of mystery, magic, and dark forces beyond our control. The question, What if we could enter a game of dark magic? has fascinated me for years and eventually became the foundation for this book.

As a composer, I've always believed that songs are stories that come to life. Likewise, *The Game of Zyphora* is a story that needed to be told. It's a journey into a world where ancient games control the fates of those who play them, where dark forces manipulate the players, and where the boundaries between the real and the imagined blur.

This book is not just about magic; it's about choices, destiny, and the forces that draw us into their games. I hope that as you read, you'll find yourself drawn into this world, questioning what's real and wondering what happens when you play a game that controls everything.

Thank you for joining me on this journey. I hope you enjoy this adventure as much as I enjoyed writing it.

Hook

"The Game of Zyphora was never meant to be played. It was a curse, a trap woven into the fabric of time itself, waiting for the right moment to claim its players. Now, Iniyan and Shifali have crossed the line, drawn in by whispers of an ancient power that calls to them in the dark. But as time slips away, the question remains: will they escape the game's grasp, or will they become part of its twisted history, lost forever?"

About The Author

I'm Keerthana Ramkumar, a passionate composer and storyteller.

I've always believed that stories are the heart of everything we do. I love composing songs because, to me, every song tells a story. I find beauty in mystery and magic, which often leads me to wonder—what if we could step into a game of dark magic? This thought lingered in my mind for a long time, and it eventually grew into my novel, *The Game of Zyphora.*

I did my BSc in Visual Communication, which kickstarted my journey into scriptwriting. It all began when I wrote my own story for a college project, and that's when the idea for *Zyphora* was born—back then, it was called *Checkmate.* After five years of contemplation, I decided to revisit and transform that original story into this novel, which I am thrilled to present to you now.

Though *Zyphora* was my first story, I ventured into other narratives along the way, and my debut novel, The *Game of Strings,* was one I completed fully. It's a story that taught me a lot about perseverance and the power of creativity. I've also written several other stories that might one day see the light of day, but for now, I hope you enjoy this one.

The first book I ever read was *I Too Had a Love Story* by Ravinder Singh, and it remains one of my favorite books to this day. It inspired me to pursue my love for storytelling. My favorite genres are love, mystery, fantasy, and adventure—stories that transport you to different worlds, much like the one I've created in *The Game of Zyphora.*

I hope my stories bring as much joy to you as they do to me when I write them, and I look forward to sharing many more in the future.

CHAPTER ONE

THE LENS OF UNSEEN REALMS

Our story begins with a woman named Shifali, someone whose curiosity knew no limits. She was the kind of person who didn't just look at the world—she dissected it, understood it, and sought to reveal its hidden truths. While others saw only the surface, Shifali always believed there was more beneath it, just waiting to be discovered.

From a young age, she was fascinated by the idea that there were forces and patterns invisible to the human eye, yet shaping everything around her. As a child, she spent hours experimenting with gadgets, dismantling toys, and reading science books that spoke of mysterious fields and quantum realms. By the time she reached her twenties, she had turned her obsession into a passion—she wanted to invent something that could allow her to see what no one else could.

"People think I'm crazy," she often said with a smile, her fingers working busily on a half-finished projcct. "But I know there's something more to this world. I can feel it."

Shifali was a contradiction in the best possible way. Modern or traditional? Both. Outside, she embraced her roots—soft, earthy shawls draped over her shoulders, vibrant kurtas paired with delicate bangles, and neatly tied hair that reflected her respect for simplicity and culture. She moved through the streets like a breeze—quiet, unassuming, blending into the fabric of her traditional surroundings. People admired her gentle demeanor, mistaking it for meekness, not realizing there was fire beneath her calm surface.

But once she stepped inside her lab, Shifali transformed into someone else entirely. The shawl was the first to go, hung neatly near the door. Loose shirts and worn jeans replaced her traditional attire—practical clothing that allowed her to crawl under tables, adjust machinery, and work with delicate instruments without restraint. Her hair, tied back hastily, often fell into unruly strands framing her face, too stubborn to stay out of her way. The bangles were exchanged for a worn-out leather band on her wrist, marked with ink stains from scribbled notes on energy patterns and complex equations.

Shifali's desk was a mix of modern science and ancient mysticism. A laptop sat next to old books filled with cryptic symbols and formulas. Her workspace was cluttered with tools—precision screwdrivers, copper wires, and vials of glowing liquids. Dim candles flickered beside stacks of research papers, while strange artifacts and crystal shards filled the corners of the room. The air was a blend of burnt incense and metal, creating an atmosphere where science and dark magic seemed to collide. It was the perfect place for Shifali's latest project—a creation that bridged both worlds.

Her latest obsession? A lens. Not just any ordinary lens, but one that could reveal the hidden dimensions, energies, and forces that pulsed through all living things, through every object, and even the very air.

The village Shifali had moved to was called Vridhaapur. It was a place that seemed untouched by time, where ancient traditions mingled with the whispers of forgotten legends. The cobblestone streets, old stone houses, and the overgrown greenery gave it a timeless aura, almost as if the village held secrets from a bygone era.

Shifali had arrived here two years ago, searching for peace and solitude after the chaos of the city. But it was in Vridhaapur that her lens project was born. The village's quiet, mysterious atmosphere and the strange energy that seemed to pulse beneath its surface inspired her to dive deeper into the unknown, setting her on the path to uncovering the hidden forces of the world.

Shifali spent months in her small lab, a cluttered room filled with books, wires, and half-finished projects. Each day was consumed with tinkering, testing, and refining her invention. She knew the challenges were enormous—there were theories to prove, materials to perfect, and designs to make—but she refused to give up. She was determined to bring her vision to life.

One evening, as she sat hunched over her workbench, soldering a delicate wire to the lens, she muttered to herself, "This is it... this is the breakthrough I've been waiting for."

Her hands trembled slightly as she placed the final piece onto the device. She leaned back, staring at the lens in front of her. It looked simple, but she knew better. The possibilities that lay within were endless.

Shifali took a deep breath. "Here goes nothing."

She slid the lens over her eyes, adjusting the focus. She blinked once, then twice. And then... nothing. For a moment, she thought it hadn't worked. But then, she felt something. It was like the lens was suddenly connected to everything around her. The world seemed clearer, sharper—like she could see things in a way she never had before.

"Wow," she whispered to herself, amazed. "This is... incredible."

She grabbed her phone, eager to share her discovery. There was only one person she knew who would understand her excitement. Iniyan. He was her closest friend, and while he had a different perspective on life—he was more grounded and logical—he always appreciated Shifali's thirst for discovery.

She dialed his number quickly, barely able to contain her enthusiasm.

"Iniyan!" she said when he picked up. "You won't believe what I've done. I've created it—the lens. It actually works!"

Iniyan's voice sounded amused but curious. "Wait, hold on. What lens? Is this like the 'energy lens' you were always talking about? What does it do?"

"Yes, exactly!" Shifali replied, her voice rising with excitement. "It's not just a regular lens. It shows you—well, I don't even know how to explain it. You have to see it for yourself."

Iniyan paused for a moment before responding. "That sounds amazing. But, listen, I just came to my Ammama's place. She asked me to stay here for a couple of days. Why don't you come over here instead?"

Shifali hesitated for a moment, then smiled. "Ammama's place, huh? Alright, I'll be there soon. Let me get this lens packed up."

"Great! I'll be waiting," Iniyan said, his voice lighter now. "But just so you know, I'm skeptical. You better show me some real magic."

Shifali laughed, excitement bubbling up again. "You'll see, Iniyan. This isn't just magic, it's science!"

As she hung up, Shifali's heart raced with anticipation. She couldn't wait for Iniyan to see the lens. She packed it carefully, making sure it was safe for the journey, and headed out, eager to reveal her invention to her closest friend. This was the beginning of something big, something that could change everything. But little did they know, the discovery was just the beginning of a journey neither of them was prepared for.

CHAPTER TWO

THE SILENT SECRET

The evening had settled into a hushed quiet, a kind of stillness that only came to Iniyan's grandmother's house. Located at the edge of a village where stories lived longer than the people who told them, the house itself seemed alive—its creaks whispering secrets of old.

Iniyan sat by the low wooden table in the main hall, fiddling with a pocket watch he had found earlier that day. It had stopped working long ago, but he liked the way it felt in his hands—timeless yet broken.

This was his world. A world of calm and quiet, where things moved slowly and nothing ever seemed to change. And yet, as he sat there, his mind drifted to something else. A place far from here. A world of excitement. Games. Challenges. Something more than this tranquil life.

This is our Iniyan, someone who wasn't afraid of the unknown, someone who sought the thrill of new experiences and adventures. He wasn't the type to sit idly for too long. Games—whether they were physical or mental—had always been his thing. He could spend hours figuring out puzzles, analyzing strategies, or playing board games with his friends.

Iniyan was the type of person who kept things simple. He didn't need fancy clothes or extravagant accessories. His everyday look consisted of a plain, faded t-shirt, worn jeans, and comfortable sneakers, all reflecting his practical nature. His hair was neatly combed back, always with a quick swipe of his hand. Despite the simplicity, there was an undeniable charm about his effortless style—a sense of someone who was grounded, yet always ready for the next adventure.

To Iniyan, life was a series of challenges to be conquered. But at that moment, as he stared at the still pocket watch, he realized something. Life here, in this small village, wasn't offering him the thrill he craved.

There had to be more.

Iniyan had come to Vridhaapur for one reason—his grandmother. The village, with its old stories and even older secrets, was where she had lived for years, far from the bustling life he knew. It was quiet, peaceful, and familiar. He hadn't expected much excitement when he arrived, but he was also eager to reconnect with Shifali, who had settled in this village too. It had been some time since they last spoke, and Iniyan was looking forward to catching up with her. The village, with its mysteries, felt like the perfect backdrop for the reunion. Little did he know, the peaceful serenity of Vridhaapur would soon give way to the unknown.

Across from him, his grandmother—Ammama—rocked gently in her chair, her shawl wrapped snugly around her thin shoulders. The flickering kerosene lamp in the corner of the room cast elongated shadows on the walls.

"Iniyan kutta," Ammama began suddenly, her voice steady and soft, "you're too curious for your own good."

Iniyan looked up, flashing his boyish grin. "Isn't that a good thing, Ammama? Curiosity leads to discoveries, doesn't it?"

Ammama's gaze was sharp despite her years. "Some discoveries are better left untouched, unspoken... unseen."

Her tone made Iniyan pause. He watched as her wrinkled hands traced a faint pattern on the armrest of her chair, as though she were writing invisible symbols into the air.

"What are you talking about, Ammama?" he asked, curious despite himself.

Ammama sighed, the sound heavy with memory. "Let me tell you a story, kutta. But it's not just any story—it's about a game. A game that doesn't just test your skills, but your soul."

Iniyan straightened up, setting the pocket watch aside. Ammama only told stories like this when the night was quiet and the wind outside carried secrets.

"Once, in a kingdom long forgotten by time, there was a land called Zyphora," she began, her voice low and steady, as though she feared the story might awaken something. "Zyphora was a place of beauty and magic, where kings ruled and sorcerers whispered spells. But their thirst for power was endless."

The king of that land, Draegor, wanted more than power; he wanted immortality, control over all men. And to get it, he sought the help of a sorcerer named...

She paused, the name lingering on her lips like a curse. "Vraxen."

"Vraxen," Iniyan repeated, a chill settling into the room.

"Vraxen wasn't just any sorcerer, kutta. He was a master of curses, a weaver of fates. He promised Draegor the ultimate weapon—a chessboard carved from obsidian and moonlight crystal, alive with magic. But it wasn't just a board. It was a trap, a cage for souls."

Iniyan frowned. "How can a chessboard trap souls?"

Ammama leaned forward, her voice dipping into a whisper. "Because the pieces weren't just wood or stone. They were living, breathing entities, born from dark magic. The Black King held a gem in his crown—a green stone that pulsed with energy. That gem wasn't just for show, Iniyan. It was the heart of the game, the source of its power."

Iniyan swallowed, his throat dry. "What happened to Draegor?"

Ammama's eyes never left his. "The first time he played, he lost."

He blinked. "But it's just a game—"

"No, kutta," Ammama interrupted, her tone sharp. "It was never just a game. Draegor didn't realize the board demanded something in return. When he lost, his soul was claimed, and his body became nothing but dust. His spirit... bound to the board forever. And Vraxen? He vanished, leaving behind the cursed board that no one could destroy."

Iniyan shivered. The flickering flame of the lamp threw shadows across Ammama's face, making her look older than her years. "So... what happened to the board?"

"It disappeared," Ammama said, her voice now barely audible, as if the story itself were listening. "Some say it was hidden deep beneath the earth. Others believe it waits in dark corners, calling out to the curious, the brave, and the foolish."

"Calling out?" Iniyan whispered, his heart pounding.

"Yes," Ammama said, her voice a faint echo. "The game chooses its players. It pulls them in, makes them part of its world. And once you start playing..." she paused, "...there's no escape until the game ends."

A silence stretched between them, broken only by the distant howl of the wind outside. Iniyan licked his lips nervously. "But that's just a story, Ammama. Right?"

Ammama didn't answer immediately. She rocked back and forth slowly, her gaze distant. Finally, she looked at him, her expression unreadable. "Kutta, stories are born from truths that people fear to accept. I'm telling you this because curiosity runs deep in our family. If you ever find something that feels alive—like a board, a game, or anything that calls to you—leave it alone. Not everything that shines is meant to be touched."

Iniyan nodded, though a lingering thrill remained at the back of his mind. A cursed game. A story of magic, power, and lost souls. It sounded impossible... but something about the way Ammama told it made it feel too real.

Ammama leaned back, the rocking chair creaking softly. "Now go to bed, Iniyan. It's late."

As Iniyan stood up, he hesitated. "Ammama... what was the name of the board?"

She looked up at him, her eyes shadowed by the lamplight. "The Game of Zyphora."

As Iniyan lay in bed that night, Ammama's words refused to leave him. Somewhere deep in the shadows of forgotten places, the Game of Zyphora waited—alive, hungry, and calling out to the curious.

And curiosity, after all, was Iniyan's greatest weakness.

CHAPTER THREE

THE WHISPERS OF THE DARK

The room was quiet, the only sound the faint rustle of the wind outside. Iniyan lay in his bed, the cool sheets wrapped around him as he stared at the ceiling, his mind still swirling with Ammama's tale. Zyphora, Draegor, Vraxen—the ancient game. The whispers of a world far beyond his own had filled his thoughts. He couldn't shake the feeling that something deep inside him was calling, urging him to uncover the mystery.

And then, just as he began to drift into sleep, it came. A voice.

"Iniyan..."

The whisper was soft, like a breath against his ear. It wasn't a voice he recognized. He sat up abruptly, his heart racing. The room was dark, save for the faint slivers of moonlight peeking through the curtains. The air seemed heavier now, charged with an invisible energy.

He shook his head, trying to shake off the unsettling feeling, but the whisper came again—closer, clearer this time.

"We have chosen you, Iniyan."

His breath caught in his throat. It wasn't just a whisper now; the voice seemed to surround him, filling the room with a soft, almost hypnotic echo.

"You are the one. You have the power to end the curse."

The words wrapped around him like a thick fog. He blinked, his pulse quickening. The room felt as though it was closing in on him. His mind swirled with confusion and intrigue. The curse? What curse? What power?

"Only you can break the chains. Only you can stop the darkness. The Game has been set, and you are its key."

His body felt stiff, the words seeping into his mind like poison. How could this be real? he thought. But the voice, the whisper, it felt so convincing. It felt so right. His mind was racing, spinning, grasping at the possibility that maybe... just maybe... this was real. Maybe he was meant for something greater.

The voice deepened, now resonating with an eerie, seductive confidence.

"You will save us, Iniyan. You will save yourself. You must come. We need you."

Iniyan's hand trembled as he pushed himself up, swinging his legs off the bed. His mind was in a haze, caught between fear and fascination. He couldn't think clearly, the pull of the whispers growing stronger, louder. The words were seeping into his bones, telling him that he was chosen, that he had been destined for this moment.

"The Game waits for you. Your move will change everything."

He stood, feet moving before his mind could catch up, as if his body were acting of its own accord. His heart thudded loudly in his chest, the weight of the whispers pressing down on him, making him feel as though he had no choice, as though he needed to follow.

But then, just as he reached for the door, something inside him snapped. The whispers weren't real. They were trying to manipulate him, to drag him into something he couldn't understand. He stumbled back, his mind slowly clearing.

"You think you can resist?" The voice was now tinged with malice, as if it could sense his hesitation. "You are the chosen one, Iniyan. You cannot escape this fate. The Game is yours."

But Iniyan gritted his teeth. He could feel the weight of the whispers pressing against his thoughts, but he forced himself to focus. His breath was shallow, his pulse racing, but he wasn't going to let the voice win. Not this time.

"No," he muttered under his breath. "I won't listen to you."

The voice faltered for a moment, then softened, as if it were coaxing him again.

"You think you can escape the curse? You think you can run from what you are?"

Iniyan's head spun. The whispers continued, growing more desperate, more frantic, as if trying to pull him in. But he clenched his fists, standing firm. The whispers were just illusions, tricks, meant to break him down. He wouldn't fall for it.

And then, just as quickly as they had come, the whispers began to fade, their voices dissipating into the darkness. The room grew still again, the tension lifting.

He stood there for a moment, breathless, his body trembling with adrenaline. His mind was clouded with questions. What had just happened? Was the curse real? Was the Game real? But even as he questioned, part of him felt a sense of resolve. He wasn't going to let some voice in the night control him.

Slowly, he returned to his bed, but the whispers still lingered in his mind, like a faint, unsettling hum.

As he lay back down, his thoughts raced. The whispers had promised him something—power, purpose, a way to end a curse. But at what cost? And who had sent them?

With a deep breath, Iniyan closed his eyes, the echoes of the whispers still swirling in his mind, but this time, he didn't give in. He would find the answers, but he would do it on his own terms.

The night was silent again, but the seed of doubt had been planted. And somewhere deep inside, Iniyan knew that whatever this Game was, it wasn't over yet.

CHAPTER FOUR

The Call of the Game

The sun had barely risen, casting a soft golden glow over the world outside, as Iniyan woke up to the gentle hum of the morning. His head still buzzed with the remnants of the night's strange whispers. He rubbed his eyes, trying to shake off the feeling of unease that clung to him. It had been a restless night, filled with echoes of voices that shouldn't have been there.

The house was quiet, except for the soft clinking of plates from the kitchen. As Iniyan dragged himself out of bed and walked towards the window, the sunlight warmed his face, but the unease lingered. His mind replayed the whispers—chosen one, the game, the curse. Could it all have been just his imagination? Or had something darker begun to stir?

Before he could dwell on it any longer, there was a knock on the door.

Iniyan opened it to find Shifali standing there, her usual confident smile replaced by a look of excitement and urgency. She was holding a small, intricate device in her hand, something that resembled a pair of glasses with strange, glowing lenses.

"Iniyan!" Shifali burst into the room, her voice full of excitement. "I've found something. Something unbelievable."

Iniyan looked up from his chair, his eyes narrowing with curiosity. "Unbelievable? You mean... the lens, right? You told me about it yesterday."

Shifali nodded quickly, her energy infectious. "Yes, the lens! But this... this is different. I've seen something with it, something I can't explain. Something... strange."

Iniyan set down the book he was holding, intrigued. "Okay, you've got my attention. What did you find?"

She paced around the room, clearly trying to collect her thoughts. "Well, yesterday, I was on my way here, and I decided to wear the lens just to test it more. You know, I saw the energy around me—everything has its own energy, right? People, objects... It was amazing, Iniyan. Everything was glowing with this energy I could see so clearly."

Iniyan leaned forward, his curiosity peaked. "That's... sounds cool. But you said you found something strange, right?"

Shifali stopped pacing and looked at him seriously, her expression darkening. "Yeah. As I was driving, I felt something... different. At first, I thought it was just a glitch or something, but then I saw it—a dark energy. It wasn't like the others. It was like it was... watching me. And it wasn't just in the background, you know? It felt like it was calling me, pulling me."

Iniyan's brows furrowed, and he felt a shiver run down his spine. "Calling you? What do you mean by that?"

Shifali continued, her voice low. "I don't know why, but I followed it. It led me to something... a gameboard. It looked ancient, but it was so beautiful, so captivating. The kind of thing you can't just walk past, you know? It was like it wanted me to take it."

Iniyan stood up, his mind racing. "A gameboard? You just... took it with you?"

Shifali nodded, her eyes wide with both excitement and confusion. "Yeah, I brought it home. I couldn't resist. There was something about it. The energy around it was so strong, so... alive. It was like it was waiting for me. I've been studying it since, and... I think this game, this board, is something far bigger than we realize."

Iniyan took a step back, trying to process her words. "So, you found this gameboard, and now you think it's connected to something... big?"

She paused for a moment, as if weighing her next words carefully. "Yes I think... it's connected to something bigger. Something that's been hidden for centuries."

"I'm not sure what to call it yet," she said, leaning forward, her voice low with excitement. "But it was a game. An ancient game, unlike anything I've ever seen. The energy it gave off was... dark. And powerful."

Shifali took a deep breath, adjusting the lens in her hands. "I can't explain it fully, but when I wore the lens, I could see the game board. It wasn't like the games I've studied before. This one was alive—it was moving, reacting to the energy around it. Almost like it was aware of me watching."

Iniyan stared at her, trying to comprehend what she was saying. "Are you sure? It sounds... too bizarre."

Shifali nodded, her face serious now. "I'm telling you, Iniyan. This game isn't just some board with pieces. It's a living thing. The energy it exudes—it's like it's pulling you in, trying to control you. I've never felt anything like it before."

She leaned forward again, her eyes intense. "And the more I studied it, the more I realized. It's not just about the pieces. It's about the people who play it. The energy it's connected to... it has a curse."

Iniyan's mind raced. The word curse hit him like a blow. It was the same word he'd heard from his Ammama the day before and it also reminded him of the whispers he heard the night before. He felt his heart rate pick up, his curiosity piqued, but also a sense of unease creeping in.

"What do you mean by curse?" he asked cautiously.

Shifali hesitated for a moment, then spoke in a soft voice. "I think this game has been trapping people. The energy it produces—it doesn't just affect the players; it binds them to the game. And the longer they stay, the more they lose themselves. Their minds, their souls... it's like the game feeds on them."

Iniyan was silent for a moment, the weight of her words sinking in. The whispers from the night before suddenly felt all too real. His instincts told him to walk away, to ignore the pull of whatever game she was talking about. But there was also a part of him—an unfamiliar part—that wanted to know more.

Iniyan's mind whirled with possibilities. Could this be the same game from Ammama's story? Could this be what the whispers had been talking about? Was this his fate, pulling him towards something far darker than he could ever imagine?

"I also found a map," Shifali continued, her voice steady. "A map that leads to the game. And it's hidden. Protected. But I'm not sure how to get there. It's almost like the game chooses you."

Iniyan's eyes narrowed as he studied Shifali, trying to make sense of everything she had just said. "Wait... a map?

You're telling me there's a hidden map that leads to this game? How did you even find out about the map?"

Shifali exhaled sharply, brushing a strand of hair behind her ear. "I didn't find it, Iniyan. It found me."

Iniyan raised a skeptical brow. "What does that even mean?"

She took a moment, searching for the right words, her gaze distant as if replaying events in her mind. "When I brought the gameboard home, I thought I'd just inspect it, you know? I didn't touch the board much—something about them didn't feel right. But then... I opened the gameboard."

Iniyan frowned, intrigued but cautious. "What happened?"

Shifali's expression darkened, and her grip on the lens tightened. "The lens. It started glowing. On its own."

Iniyan's jaw tensed. "The lens glowed?"

Shifali nodded, her voice quiet but intense. "Yes. I'd left it on the table, but when I opened the board, the lenses lit up—this faint, strange glow. I don't know how or why, but it was like the board triggered something in them. I had to know what it meant, so I put them on again."

She hesitated for a moment, her eyes searching his face before continuing. "And that's when I saw it."

Iniyan leaned forward slightly, his curiosity outweighing his unease. "Saw what?"

"The map," Shifali said, her voice just above a whisper. "The moment I looked through the lens, the gameboard wasn't just wood anymore. Trails of light spread across it—paths, symbols, landmarks... a glowing map appeared, like it had been hidden there all along. But I could only see it through the lens."

Iniyan stared at her, trying to process what she was saying. "So the board and the lens... they're connected."

"Exactly," Shifali said, nodding. "It's like the lens unlocked something. The map was alive, Iniyan—moving, shifting, like it was leading me somewhere. It felt like... it was waiting for me."

Iniyan's brows furrowed, his mind racing. "And you didn't try to follow the map?"

Shifali shook her head. "Not yet. I didn't want to go alone. The map wasn't complete—it looked like parts of it were missing or... waiting to appear. I think there's more to this, Iniyan.

Iniyan stared at her, the pieces in his mind starting to connect in strange, unsettling ways. He exhaled slowly and ran a hand through his hair. "Shifali... I need to tell you something."

Shifali's brows furrowed, her excitement giving way to concern. "What is it?"

Iniyan hesitated, his gaze flickering toward the window before settling back on her. "Last night... I didn't sleep well. I heard something—whispers. Strange voices. I couldn't make out all the words, but it felt like they were coming from everywhere." He paused, his voice lower now. "They kept saying things like *'the chosen one,' 'the game,' and... 'the curse.'"

Shifali stared at him, her face a mix of shock and recognition. "The curse? Iniyan, do you know what you're saying?"

Iniyan nodded slowly. "I didn't think much of it at first, but... even my grandmother yesterday, told me something strange. She said there's an old story, something about a cursed game that binds people to it. She didn't go into detail, but she warned me to stay away if I ever came across anything unusual."

"I think the game chooses people. And now, it's chosen us.", says Shifali.

"Chosen us?" Iniyan repeated, skepticism heavy in his voice. "You think the game wants us to follow this map?"

"I know it sounds insane," Shifali admitted, her tone earnest, "but it's more than just a game. It's alive. I could feel it when I looked at that map—the energy, the pull. It was like it was calling me somewhere."

Iniyan turned away, staring at the sunlight pouring through the window as her words hung in the air. The weight of it all settled on his shoulders. He wanted to deny it, to walk away from whatever strange thing Shifali had discovered. But something about this—about the lens, the map, and even the unease he'd felt all morning—tugged at the back of his mind.

Finally, he turned back to her. "Alright," he said, his voice steady but cautious. "Let's follow the map. But if we're doing this, we stick together. No risks."

Shifali's face lit up with relief and determination. "Agreed."

Iniyan took the lens from her hand, its faint weight colder than he expected. As he held it, a quiet shiver ran through him. He couldn't help but feel that this was only the beginning of something far bigger than either of them could understand.

And for the first time, Iniyan wondered if they were ready for where this map would lead.

CHAPTER FIVE

AMMAMA'S WARNING

The two of them—Shifali holding the glowing lens and Iniyan feeling uneasy—made their way to Ammama's room. The old house had that familiar, comforting smell of spices and incense, but today, something felt different. The air felt heavier, as if something was waiting to be said.

Ammama was sitting in her chair, eyes closed, lost in a quiet prayer as usual. Iniyan and Shifali exchanged a glance before Iniyan spoke up.

"Ammama," he began, his voice hesitant, "Shifali found something... something strange. A game. And we need to talk to you about it."

Ammama opened her eyes slowly, peering at the two of them. Her sharp gaze seemed to pierce right through them, as if she already knew what was coming. But she said nothing, waiting for them to continue.

Shifali stepped forward, holding out the glowing lens. "This... this is what led me to the game. It's some kind of... ancient thing. When I wear it, I can see energy patterns. And I saw this game—a game that's connected to dark energy. It feels alive. Almost like it's pulling us in."

Iniyan felt a shiver run down his spine as he added, "We think this game... might be the one you warned me about. You said something would come after me. I heard whispers last night. It felt like it was calling me."

Ammama's face changed. Her expression, once calm and collected, twisted with worry. She took a deep breath, staring at the lens in Shifali's hand like it was something cursed. "No," she whispered, shaking her head slowly. "No, not that game. You shouldn't even be thinking about it."

Iniyan frowned. "But why, Ammama? What's wrong with it?"

Ammama stood up, her old bones creaking as she moved across the room. She paced for a moment, rubbing her forehead as if trying to gather her thoughts. Finally, she turned to them, her voice quiet but filled with warning. "I knew it would reach you eventually. I sensed it during my spiritual meditation. I knew it would come, and now here you are, standing right at its edge."

She walked over to her small altar, lighting a candle and bowing her head. "This game—this is no ordinary game. It isn't just about chess or strategy. It's about luck and knowledge. It's about forces that you cannot control, forces that can pull you into another world."

Iniyan and Shifali exchanged uneasy glances. Iniyan could feel his heart racing. He had thought he was just helping Shifali discover something new. But this... this was different.

Ammama's voice grew more serious, her tone sharp. "Once you are chosen, you start hearing whispers, it means it picked you, you only have 24 hours before it pulls you inside. And when you're inside... it's like you're trapped. You won't even remember the world outside. You will only focus on the game, and all I've said now? You won't remember any of it. The game will change you, make you forget everything."

Shifali opened her mouth to protest, but Ammama raised a hand. "No," she said firmly. "It will pull you in. I know it. I can feel it, and I'm telling you now: don't go near it. Don't play it. If you go inside that game, there is a chance... a big chance that you'll never come back. You'll be lost forever."

The room felt cold despite the warm sunlight outside. The weight of Ammama's words hung in the air, heavy and suffocating. Iniyan wanted to argue, to ask her more, but something in her eyes told him not to. He felt a chill run through his spine as he realized that maybe, just maybe, Ammama was right.

But then, Ammama sighed, her shoulders slumping as if the weight of the world had suddenly crushed her. "I can't stop you," she murmured. "I've seen this happen before, and I knew... I knew it would come to you. It always does. But whatever it tells you, whatever tricks it plays, don't let it win. If you're chosen, it will do everything to make you want to play. It will twist your mind, make you think it's worth it, make you think you can win."

She walked over to them slowly, her old eyes filled with concern. "But if you lose... if you fail... you'll be lost forever. There's no coming back from that. It doesn't care about you, your dreams, your life. It only cares about keeping you there."

Shifali looked down at the lens in her hands, her expression conflicted. Iniyan's mind raced with questions. Could they walk away from this? Could they ignore the whispers, the pull of the game?

"I'm telling you this, not because I want to scare you," Ammama said, her voice softer now. "But because I love you. And I know what this game can do. I can sense its power. I can feel it reaching for you already. Please, please don't go near it."

She walked to the door, her movements slow but steady. "I know it's tempting, and I know you both want to solve it, but don't. Just throw it away. Forget everything I've said and walk away while you still can."

The door closed behind her with a soft thud, leaving Iniyan and Shifali standing in the room, the air heavy with uncertainty.

Iniyan stood there, the weight of Ammama's words sinking in. His mind was a whirlwind of thoughts, the game, the lens, the curse—everything felt like it was closing in on him. Could he really walk away? Could they just let it go?

He didn't have an answer. All he knew was that the whispers, the energy, the game—it wasn't going to let them forget about it. And somehow, in the pit of his stomach, he knew that whatever choice they made next, it would change everything.

CHAPTER SIX

THE DARK INVITATION

It had been 20 hours since it had invited them. Four hours left before the curse could pull them into the game. Iniyan's mind was racing with confusion and fear. Every word Ammama said was echoing in his head, but there was something else—a pull, a temptation he couldn't ignore.

Shifali, sitting across from him, was fiddling with the lens in her hands, deep in thought. The silence in the room was heavy, both of them aware that time was running out.

"Iniyan," Shifali finally spoke, her voice soft but determined, "We can't just wait here for the time to run out. We have to act, we need to figure out more about this game."

Iniyan looked at her but said nothing. His mind was elsewhere, still replaying the warnings Ammama had given them.

"Where's the gameboard?" he asked, his voice almost mechanical as he tried to push his fears aside.

"I kept it at my place," Shifali answered, her gaze falling on the lens in her hands. "But—"

"Let it stay there for now. We'll go there after 24 hours," Iniyan interrupted, trying to keep his thoughts straight.

He glanced at the lens again, lying on the table. Something about it was pulling him in. His hand reached out without thinking, and before he knew it, he was slipping it on his eyes.

Immediately, the world around him changed.

Colors, energy, and vibrations that were once invisible to him became starkly apparent. He could see the faint blue aura surrounding Shifali, a calm and steady energy. But when his gaze shifted to Ammama, the energy was different—strong, spiritual, and overwhelmingly positive. It was almost blinding in its purity.

But then, something else caught his attention. A dark swirl of energy, slowly rotating around Ammama. Iniyan blinked, unsure if his mind was playing tricks on him, but the energy began to focus on him. It became sharper, more defined, and then— it looked at him.

The voice that followed was chilling, slithering into his mind like a cold breeze.

"Iniyan..." the voice whispered, its tone laced with dark intent, "You love your Ammama, don't you? You want to protect her, don't you? Play the game. I'll give you the best invitation anyone has ever received."

The words sent a jolt through him. His heart raced, and his palms began to sweat. His body instinctively took a step back. But before he could react further, the energy intensified, as if beckoning him, pulling him closer.

"Come..." the voice urged again, now more insistent.

Iniyan's feet betrayed him. His body wavered, and before he could control himself, he fell backward, crashing onto the floor with a loud thud. He immediately ripped the lens off, tossing it aside, his breath coming in rapid gasps.

Ammama's voice broke through the tension, calm and steady. "Be careful, Iniyan," she said, her eyes sharp, watching him closely.

But even after he took off the lens, the dark energy still lingered in his vision. He could see the spot where it had been, still faintly glowing. His body was trembling, and his mind was clouded with uncertainty.

Suddenly, a loud noise broke the stillness. A pot, which had been sitting on a nearby shelf, crashed to the ground as if it had been pushed by an invisible force.

Iniyan's heart skipped a beat. The energy—it was real. It was more than just a trick of the lens. It could do things.

He couldn't ignore it anymore. The weight of the dark energy pulling at him, the voice calling him... he had to tell Shifali. He needed to make sure they were both on the same page. They couldn't risk losing Ammama to whatever this game was.

I can't lose her, Iniyan thought to himself as he quickly stood up. The feeling of dread gripped him. This wasn't just some game. This was something far more dangerous, and the fact that he had been marked for it, made him sick to his stomach.

He rushed to Shifali, his face pale with fear. "Shifali, listen to me. We need to stop this. The game is already reaching for us—it's real. Ammama... she's already in danger."

Shifali raised an eyebrow. "What are you talking about, Iniyan? You're scaring me."

"I saw it. The game... it's more than just a game. I felt the dark energy. It called to me. It wants me to play," Iniyan explained quickly, his voice shaky."

Iniyan stood frozen, his heart racing, sweat trickling down his temple. His hands trembled as he gripped the lens, still half in his mind, trying to process everything he had just seen—the dark swirling energy, the voice that beckoned him. His breath came in short bursts as he tried to shake off the feeling that had clung to him.

Shifali, however, remained calm, though she could see the fear in his eyes. She took a step closer to him, her hand gently resting on his arm, trying to ground him in the moment.

"Iniyan," she said softly, "It's okay. We still have time. We haven't crossed the line yet."

Her words were like a small anchor, pulling him back from the edge of his panic. But still, doubt gnawed at him. Is it really is coming for us?

"But what if it's just scaring us, Shifali?" Iniyan asked, his voice trembling. He looked over at her, desperately searching for some reassurance. "What if we're overreacting? It could just be tricks... tricks to make us think it's real."

Shifali gave a small shrug, her face thoughtful. "I don't know, Iniyan. Maybe. But... what if it's not? We've already felt its presence. We've seen the strange energy around us. The lens shows things we can't ignore."

She gave a deep sigh, not knowing herself what the true answer was, but trying to make sense of the uncertainty. "Maybe it's trying to get inside our heads. Maybe it's not dangerous... yet. But we still don't know enough. We're on the edge of something, and I don't think we can just walk away from it without understanding what it really is."

Iniyan ran a hand through his hair, frustrated. "I'm not sure I can handle this. I don't want to lose Ammama, but also I don't want us to be trapped in some game we don't understand."

Shifali stepped back slightly, her eyes narrowing as she studied him. "You're not going to lose anyone, Iniyan. We still have time. We can figure this out. We don't have to play the game just because it want us to."

The fear and hesitation in his chest didn't fade. He knew Shifali was right—there was still time—but every second that passed made it harder to ignore the sensation that they were being watched, that the game was already trying to pull them in. But as Shifali said, they hadn't crossed that line yet. They could still turn back if they made the right choice.

But deep down, a part of him feared that the choice might not be theirs to make.

"I don't know, Shifali," he whispered, more to himself than to her. "Something about this feels different... more dangerous. More real."

Shifali watched him, her expression softening. She understood his fear, but there was something inside her—a curiosity, an excitement—that pushed her to keep going. "We'll figure it out. You're not alone in this. Whatever happens, we'll face it together."

Iniyan wanted to believe her, but the tension in the room had shifted, like the air before a storm. He glanced back at the lens on the table, then to the window, where the fading light of the day seemed to whisper its own warning.

He wasn't sure what would happen next, but he couldn't shake the feeling that time was slipping away faster than they could stop it.

CHAPTER SEVEN

THE PAUSE BEFORE THE STORM

Thirty minutes. That's all they had left. Iniyan sat, staring at the clock. Each tick felt like a countdown to something bigger, something more intense. The second hand moved slower than usual, almost as if it was dragging its feet. He glanced at Shifali, whose face was a mirror of his own confusion. She was staring at the clock, too, waiting for the moment to strike.

Then, it happened.

Everything stopped.

The air felt heavier, thicker. It wasn't just the clock. It was the entire world. The hum of traffic outside, the wind outside rustling the leaves—it all went dead silent. Iniyan blinked, trying to make sense of what was happening. He looked at Shifali. Her eyes were wide, her mouth slightly open in shock. She was frozen in time, just like him.

"Iniyan," she said, her voice shaking, "What the hell is happening?"

He couldn't answer. He didn't know what was going on. But he could feel it in his bones—something bigger than them was at play. The game. The energy. The curse.

He took a step forward, feeling like he was walking through a dream. Every movement was deliberate, slow, as if he was underwater. He glanced back at the clock, still frozen at 08:30 PM. It was like time itself had just...paused.

"We need to go to Ammama," Iniyan said, his voice sounding distant in the stillness of the world.

They rushed to Ammama's room, but she, too, was frozen. Her hands were still, her eyes wide but lifeless. Nothing moved. Iniyan's heart raced. It was like the universe was holding its breath, waiting for something to happen.

"Why is she...?" Shifali whispered, stepping forward. "What's going on?"

Iniyan shook his head. He didn't know. All he knew was that time had stopped for a reason. The game... it was here. And it was calling them.

A few minutes passed, or maybe it was longer—who could tell when time didn't exist? They stood there, in stunned silence, the weight of the moment pressing down on them.

"This is it, isn't it?" Shifali said, her voice breaking the silence. "The game is pulling us in. It's happening now."

Iniyan looked at her, his mind racing. He could feel the pressure of the countdown still hanging over him. They had only 30 minutes, but in this strange, frozen world, it felt like hours had passed. He could hear the whispers again, the voice tempting him, pulling him toward the game.

"We have to go," he said, his voice steady now, though his hands were shaking. "We have no choice."

Shifali nodded, determination settling over her face. "Let's get the game. If we're going to play, we do it on our terms."

They walked to the door, every step feeling unnatural in the silence. Iniyan felt a strange tug in his chest, the knowledge that the game was waiting for them. Waiting to pull them in. Waiting to test them.

They walked down the hallway, their footsteps echoing in the quiet house. There was no sound, no outside world to distract them. Just them, walking towards their fate.

As they approached the door, Iniyan stopped for a moment, looking back at Ammama. She was still. Unmoved. He wondered if she could feel it too, wherever she was in her frozen state.

They reached Shifali's house.

Their footsteps slowing as they approached the door. The stillness lingered, an eerie quiet wrapping around them like a blanket. Shifali unlocked the door and stepped inside first, her movements sharp and deliberate. Iniyan followed, his senses heightened. Every creak of the floorboards beneath their feet seemed magnified in the silence.

But when they entered the room where she had left the gameboard, they both stopped in their tracks.

The gameboard was gone.

"What the...?" Shifali muttered, her voice filled with shock. She spun around, scanning every inch of the room as if it might appear. "I left it right here, Iniyan! I'm sure of it."

Iniyan's heart dropped, the unease curling into something sharper—fear. "You're absolutely sure? No one else could've moved it?"

"No one," Shifali said firmly. She turned to him, her face pale, but her mind was already moving. "Wait—the lens. I can use the lens."

She fumbled in her bag and pulled it out, the strange, glowing lenses flickering faintly as if they sensed what was coming. Without hesitating, she put them on, her eyes scanning the room through the glass.

For a moment, there was nothing. Just the same empty space. But then she froze.

"Iniyan," she whispered, "There's something here."

"What do you see?" he asked, stepping closer.

Shifali raised a hand, pointing to where the gameboard should've been. "It's not the gameboard... It's a map. The same map I saw before."

Iniyan's eyes widened. "The map? The one with the glowing trails?"

"Yes." Shifali's voice was tight as she studied it. "It's even clearer now—paths, symbols... like it's leading us somewhere. It's as if... the game moved itself but left the map behind for us to follow."

Iniyan swallowed hard. The pull of the game was stronger now, more deliberate, as though it was guiding them. Luring them.

"We don't have a choice," he said, his voice steady, though his nerves were fraying. "Let's follow the map. Wherever this thing is, it wants us to come to it."

Shifali nodded, slipping off the lens but keeping it close. "Let's go."

They stepped out of the house, following the paths outlined on the map. The night was dark and heavy, the air cool and eerily still. The stars above seemed too bright, as if watching them. Streetlights flickered as they passed, their glow stretching unnaturally into the darkness. It wasn't long before they found themselves on an unfamiliar road, one that seemed to appear only as they moved forward. The landscape shifted subtly, bending to the map's direction.

"What is this place?" Iniyan muttered as they walked.

Shifali shook her head. "It's like we're walking into another part of the world. Somewhere hidden."

The path led them deeper into an unfamiliar stretch of land. Time felt meaningless here; the night didn't seem to progress, and yet they walked as if for hours. Trees lined either side of the path, their branches arching like they were trying to keep something out—or maybe in.

Finally, they reached it.

A place so strange and out of place that they both stopped, stunned.

It was small yet striking, nestled in a clearing where no such place could exist. A space decorated in brilliant lights that shimmered and pulsed with life. Lanterns hung from nowhere, casting golden hues across perfectly cobbled stones. Soft, ambient music hummed faintly, like a song only the air could hear. The place seemed magical, as though it didn't belong to the world they knew.

"It's like the game owns this place," Shifali whispered, her voice filled with awe.

Iniyan stared, his gaze sweeping across the ethereal landscape. "It's... alive. The place itself."

At the center of the clearing, as if waiting for them, was a large gameboard.

The gameboard rested atop an ornate pedestal, its cover a deep, dark leather, marked only by one golden handprint.

And then they saw it.

Written in bold, ancient letters across the top of the gameboard, glowing with a strange light, were the words:

"THE GAME OF ZYPHORA."

Shifali whispered the name aloud, her voice barely audible. "*The Game of Zyphora...*"

The moment she spoke it, the letters pulsed brighter, as though the board acknowledged them.

It radiated an energy that Iniyan could feel thrumming in his chest, beckoning him.

Shifali approached it cautiously, her breath catching. "Look at this."

The golden handprints seemed to shimmer as she neared. "It's inviting us," she whispered, almost to herself. "Like it's asking us to touch it."

Iniyan's gaze flickered between her and the book. "You think... if we touch it, something happens? Like... it pulls us into the game?"

Shifali nodded, her face a mix of fear and resolve. "That's what it wants, Iniyan. I can feel it."

The air around them seemed to grow heavier as they stood there, the glowing handprints pulsing like a heartbeat. Iniyan's mind raced. This was it—the moment they would either turn back or step into the unknown.

"You don't have to do this," Iniyan said softly, though he already knew her answer.

Shifali turned to him, a flicker of a smile on her lips. "We came this far. Whatever happens next... we face it together."

Iniyan exhaled sharply, his pulse thundering in his ears. Together, they stepped forward. The book waited patiently, its glow intensifying as they reached out.

"On three?" Shifali whispered.

Iniyan nodded. "One... two..."

But Iniyan reached out first. He placed his hand on the board. It was cool to the touch, but a strange warmth radiated from it. As soon as his fingers made contact, the room seemed to explode with light.

A blinding flash engulfed them, and Iniyan felt himself pulled, as if gravity itself had turned against him. He was falling, though he didn't know where. Everything around him dissolved into a swirl of colors and shapes.

Shifali was pulled along with him, her grip tight on his hand. She didn't scream. She didn't cry. But there was an undeniable fear in her eyes. They were both caught in this whirlwind, unable to stop what was happening.

The last thing Iniyan heard before everything went dark was the soft, haunting whisper:

"Welcome to the game."

And just like that, they were gone. The gameboard, still glowing faintly, sat alone in the quiet room. The light slowly faded.

And then, silence.

The game had begun.

Back at Ammama's home, the world slowly returned to normal. The eerie stillness that had consumed everything moments ago dissipated, and time, once frozen, resumed its natural flow. The faint hum of life returned—the ticking of the clock, the distant rustle of leaves outside—but the house itself felt heavy, as though it had absorbed the lingering tension of something unnatural.

Ammama blinked, her eyes darting to the clock on the wall.

Her breath caught in her throat. The hands had aligned perfectly. The time read 9:00 PM. Exactly 24 hours had passed.

Her heart dropped. The realization hit her like a blow to the chest.

"Iniyan... Shifali..." she whispered, dread pooling in her stomach.

She moved quickly, searching the house, calling out their names as her voice echoed through the empty rooms. "Iniyan! Shifali! Where are you?"

No answer.

She checked every corner, every room, but they were gone. The house, which once felt like a place of warmth and love, now stood silent and empty. A cold chill crept up her spine as her search turned frantic.

"They can't be gone," she muttered, her voice trembling. "They can't have…"

She stopped, her hands shaking as she clutched the edge of a nearby chair to steady herself. Her gaze fell to the clock once again. Exactly 24 hours.

The whispers, the strange stillness, the warnings she had felt deep within—everything had led to this. Her worst fear had come true.

Ammama's mind raced as she stood in the deafening silence of the house. Slowly, her lips moved, barely forming the words as they escaped her.

"Could they have entered… the Game of Zyphora?"

The question hung in the air, heavy and unanswered, as the clock continued to tick.

CHAPTER EIGHT

THE MYSTERIOUS ROOM

Here's the Mysterious room.

The room was unlike anything else. It felt like a relic of a forgotten time, frozen in history. The walls, with their strange carvings, seemed to tell stories—stories of people long gone, of places that no longer existed. There was a stillness about the room, the kind of stillness that only comes with age, with time. It was almost as if the room had a life of its own, a life that stretched back centuries.

Books lined the shelves, stacked carefully, though the dust on them hinted that they hadn't been touched in years. Their leather covers were old, cracked in places, but still beautiful. Each book seemed to hold wisdom—wisdom that might never be read again. The air was thick, heavy with the scent of paper and something ancient, something untouched.

Outside, the storm raged, but the room was calm, isolated from the world outside. The only source of light came from a single, dim bulb hanging from the ceiling. Its weak glow barely reached the far corners of the room, casting long, flickering shadows on the worn wooden floor.

At the center of the room was a large chessboard. It was unlike any chessboard you'd seen before. The surface was polished, gleaming under the light of an old, antique lamp. But it wasn't just any chessboard. This one was grand, regal, as if it had seen a thousand games, each one more important than the last.

The pieces on the board were masterpieces, each one carved from rare wood, decorated with delicate gemstones. They weren't just chess pieces. They were symbols—symbols of power, of strategy, of a battle that went beyond a simple game. They stood on the board, waiting.

As you moved into the room, the atmosphere felt increasingly oppressive. There was something about this place—something unsettling. The air seemed thick, as if it was holding its breath, waiting for something to happen. Strange symbols were etched into the stone walls, symbols that seemed to shift and move when no one was looking directly at them. These weren't just random markings—they were deliberate, ancient, and held secrets that no one seemed to know.

Hidden among the books were objects that seemed out of place. Keys—large and small, each intricately designed—lay scattered across the shelves. They were beautiful but useless now, their purpose long forgotten. Along with the keys were small figurines, each carved with strange faces. There was something eerie about them, as though they were watching, waiting for something.

The room itself seemed to go on forever, twisting into hidden corners and passages that were hard to find. It was easy to get lost, and those who ventured too far would soon realize they had no idea how they had gotten there or how to leave. It wasn't a room; it was a maze, a web of time and mystery.

And then, breaking the silence, a deep voice echoed through the room. It wasn't loud, but it was commanding. "And your game starts... now."

The voice wasn't coming from anywhere in particular, yet it seemed to fill the room. It wasn't a shout, but it had the kind of power that made the walls tremble. It was as if the room itself was alive, as though it had been waiting for someone, for something, to make the first move.

In the middle of the room, the white king stood alone. It was the last piece, the only one left. Its future was uncertain, its fate hanging in the balance. Around it, the black pieces—silent, menacing—waited. They were the destroyers, the ones who would end the game if the king didn't move quickly enough. They were closing in, their black forms looming larger with every second.

The white king wasn't just a piece on a board. It was a symbol of hope, of survival. It had been through battles before, had faced odds that seemed impossible, and yet, it had stood firm. But this time, the stakes were higher. This time, the game wasn't just about winning—it was about survival. One wrong move, and the king would be lost.

The clock on the wall ticked loudly, as if reminding the king that time was running out. The sands of time were slipping away, and with each passing second, the pressure mounted. The king knew that it had to act, but how? Every move was a risk. One wrong decision, one misstep, and the game would be over.

The king surveyed the board, its mind racing, its thoughts a whirlwind. It analyzed each piece, each position, each possible outcome. It was a game of patience, a game of precision. It was a game of life and death.

50

CHAPTER NINE

THE SILENT GAME

The heavy, antique door creaked open, revealing a pitch dark room. A lone figure, a young boy, stepped cautiously into a dark room.

The room was a void, a black hole that threatened to swallow him whole. The only sound was the echo of his own ragged breath, a haunting melody that filled the silence.

Panic surged through him, a wild, untamed beast that clawed at his mind. He was trapped, a prisoner in his own fear. The darkness, a malevolent force, seemed to grow denser with each passing moment.

He stumbled forward, his outstretched hands groping for something, anything, to break the suffocating darkness. But there was nothing. The room was empty, a barren wasteland.

A cold sweat broke out on his forehead. His heart pounded in his chest, a frantic rhythm that mirrored the chaos within him. He was alone, utterly alone, a solitary figure in a vast, empty room.

A sob escaped his lips, a sound of despair and helplessness. He was lost, adrift in a sea of darkness. The fear was overwhelming, a monster that threatened to consume him.

He closed his eyes, trying to shut out the darkness, to escape the nightmare. But it was futile. The darkness was inside him, a part of him.

The boy, a figure shrouded in mystery, cautiously stepped into the inky blackness. As he moved, an invisible force seemed to work parallel to him. It was as if an unseen force was following his every move. As he took a step foward, a corresponding event unfolded in another, equally in the mysterious room.

As the boy moved, so too did the white king on the chessboard, mirroring his step in the mysterious room. The two were connected, bound by an invisible thread that stretched across the void between them.

The sound was deafening. A loud, echoing BANG filled the room, like someone had slammed a heavy iron door shut. The boy, frozen in his steps, felt his heart almost leap out of his chest.

He spun around, expecting to see the door still there, but his worst fear came true—it wasn't.

The door that he had walked through, the only way out, was gone. The wall where it had been was now smooth and unbroken, as if the door had never existed.

He took a step back, his breathing shallow. What the hell just happened?

And then, something even stranger appeared. Blood-red letters began to spread across the wall, like paint dripping down. They formed words, big and bold:

"NO EXIT."

The boy's stomach turned. It felt like someone had punched him in the gut. He swallowed hard and forced himself to look away from the wall.

He turned back to the front, strained his eyes, trying to pierce the darkness, but it was futile. The room was a void, a black hole that threatened to swallow him whole.

The chessboard in the mysterious room was glowing softly.

And then, all of a sudden, as if by magic,

Slowly, the check square the King was on before in the mysterious room vanishes, as if it had never been there. It was like a magic trick, a disappearing act on the chessboard.

But it didn't stop there. The square the boy had just stood on before also disappears.

54

CHAPTER TEN

The Horse and the Knight

The sun was unforgiving. It hung high in the sky, beating down on the vast, empty plain like a giant torch. The heat was unbearable, but it didn't seem to bother the black horse galloping across the land. It was magnificent, a creature of pure power and grace. Its coat, a deep shade of black, shimmered under the harsh sunlight. The stallion's mane flew wild behind it, a dark blur against the barren landscape.

It ran fast, faster than anything else on that plain. The hooves pounded against the dry earth with a rhythm that seemed to shake the ground beneath. The horse was free, it seemed—free to run, free to roam the endless plains without a care in the world. But that freedom was about to be shattered.

A gust of wind, sudden and strong, swept across the plain, carrying with it a crimson shawl from a nearby tent. The shawl, bright and red against the muted brown of the earth, was pulled from its resting place. It flew through the air, as if caught in the wind's wild dance. The horse didn't see it coming, and the next moment, the shawl landed right on its face.

The horse froze, momentarily disoriented. The bright red fabric, now hanging over its eyes, blocked its vision. The powerful creature snorted and tossed its head, trying to shake off the shawl. But the fabric clung to it, caught in the wild wind, and the horse struggled against the sudden restriction. The once vibrant zymbol of freedom—this shawl now became a prison, a barrier that kept the horse from seeing the path ahead.

It was as if time slowed. The world around the horse seemed to vanish, leaving only the red shawl and the heat of the sun. The animal stood still for a moment, unsure. But it couldn't afford to stand still. The wind, the horse's breathing, the sound of the hooves on the ground—everything seemed to intensify. There were two paths ahead, two ways it could go. But the horse couldn't see them clearly, not with the shawl blinding it.

One path was dark and foreboding, a road that led to uncertainty, to danger. The other was more open, a safer path, but it seemed to offer no freedom. It felt like a decision the horse should make. The animal's instincts were sharp, its body alert, but it was caught between the two roads.

Back in the mysterious room, something equally strange was happening. The chessboard, which had been quiet until now, seemed to come to life. A dim light flickered in the room, casting long shadows across the walls. And in the middle of the board, sitting like a statue, was the black knight. It was a piece of carved wood, dark and imposing against the pale squares. To anyone else, it would look like just a simple piece in a game. But there was something more to it now.

The knight on the board wasn't just a piece anymore. Its eyes, carved into the wood, seemed to glow with an eerie light. It wasn't just sitting there anymore; it was watching. It was aware of something, something beyond the confines of the board. It was connected to the horse out on the plain, somehow. As the horse struggled with the red shawl, the knight seemed to sense it, feel it. They were two separate things, worlds apart, yet their fates were tied together.

The horse's struggle with the shawl mirrored the black knight's stillness on the board. It was as if both were waiting, caught in a moment of suspended tension. The pieces were in place. The move had to be made, but neither the knight nor the horse could act until something changed, until they both understood what needed to be done.

It was a strange connection, one that couldn't be explained. It was as if the chessboard and the plain were two sides of the same coin. The moves on one side echoed on the other. The knight was waiting for its moment to spring into action, and so was the horse. Both were part of a larger game, one that was just beginning to unfold.

But what move would they make?

CHAPTER ELEVEN

THE DARK PATH AHEAD

The boy stood frozen, his breath shallow in the eerie silence. The room was pitch dark, with no clue of where he was or what he should do. His heart raced as he squinted into the void, hoping for something—anything—that would make sense of this place.

Out of nowhere, a faint flicker broke the darkness. A dim bulb on the ceiling sputtered to life, its weak light barely enough to illuminate the area around him. It flickered like it couldn't decide whether to stay on or give up entirely.

And then, it happened.

A red shawl floated down from above, drifting slowly, almost like it was caught in an invisible breeze. It landed gently on the floor, just one square in front of him.

The boy stared at it, his heart pounding. The bulb above him, which had been flickering non-stop, suddenly stopped. Now it glowed steadily, casting its faint light directly onto the shawl. It was almost as if the light was pointing at it, highlighting its importance.

He didn't move. The shawl lay perfectly still on the floor, bright red against the dullness of the room. Something about it felt off, like it was waiting for him.

It seemed strange, like it was waiting for him to touch it, to do something. The shawl, vibrant against the blackness of the room, was an invitation. But an invitation to what? He didn't know. The room felt wrong, like something dangerous was just on the other side of his thoughts, ready to pounce.

The boy swallowed hard, his throat dry. Should he pick it up? Should he even go near it? His mind raced with questions, but no answers came.

Tentatively, he took a step forward. The room felt heavier, the air thicker, as he moved closer. His instincts told him to back away, but curiosity—or maybe something stronger—pushed him on.

When he was close enough, he crouched down, hesitating. The shawl shimmered faintly under the weak bulb, its silky fabric looking harmless. But his gut told him this wasn't just any shawl.

His hands trembled as he reached down and picked up the shawl. The moment his fingers brushed the fabric, a strange sensation passed through him. The world seemed to warp, shift, and the air around him turned cold. A voice, deep and echoing, filled the room.

"You've awakened something you cannot control," the voice boomed, filling the space with a terrifying certainty.

The boy froze. He looked around but saw no one. The voice seemed to be coming from the darkness itself. He didn't know if it was real or just a trick of his mind, but it didn't matter. Fear gripped him, and he felt the weight of it in his chest. Something had begun, something beyond his control.

The shawl he had been holding in his hands suddenly crumbled away like dust, vanishing into the air. The boy was left standing in the silence, alone. He felt powerless, a pawn in a game he didn't understand. The room felt like a trap, and he was its prey.

Outside, on a vast plain, a horse stood, its breath coming in sharp, ragged bursts. Its muscles were tense, its hooves stamping on the ground. It was ready to run, ready to face whatever lay ahead.

And then, something strange happened. The crimson shawl that had been draped over its face, blocking its vision, suddenly fluttered free. It rose into the air for a brief moment, almost as if caught in an unseen wind, before falling gracefully to the ground beside the stallion. The fabric was soft, yet it seemed to pulse with an eerie energy.

The horse blinked, its vision now clear. Its head jerked up, and its gaze locked onto the path ahead.

To the right, the path was dark, twisting into an ominous forest. Shadows stretched across the ground like twisted fingers, reaching out to grab hold. The air was thick with tension, as though something was waiting just beyond the tree line. The path seemed to promise both danger and opportunity—an adventure that could either end in disaster or lead to something unimaginable.

A sudden gust of wind whipped across the plain, carrying with it a chilling whisper. The horse's ears perked up, its eyes darting around, searching for the source of the sound. A low growl echoed through the air, a sound that sent shivers down its spine.

As the horse readied itself to sprint, a strange sensation washed over it.

Meanwhile, in a dimly lit room, a chessboard sat illuminated. A lone knight, a dark figure against the pale squares, readied itself for its move. Its eyes, glowing with a sinister light, were fixed on the path the horse was about to take. The knight, a harbinger of doom, was poised to strike.

The horse, its heart pounding in its chest, pushed itself to its limits. It had to reach the end of the path, to escape the clutches of darkness. But the darkness was gaining on it, creeping closer with each passing moment. The pounding of hooves echoed in the distance, growing louder with every passing second.

The knight on the chessboard made its move, advancing towards the white king. The king, a symbol of hope and righteousness, stood his ground, his face etched with determination. The fate of the white king hung in the balance.

On the other side of the room, the boy felt his heart race.

The dim, oppressive light of the room cast long shadows, wrapping itself around him like a suffocating blanket. The sounds around him grew louder—distant whispers, scraping noises, and the slow, deliberate movements of something coming closer.

The boy, sensing the impending danger, pressed his hands to his ears, trying to block out the terrifying sounds. A cold sweat broke out on his forehead as he realized that he was not alone in this dark, desolate place. Something, or someone, was hunting him.

The sound of the hooves grew louder, closer. The boy's heart pounded in his chest, his breath quickening. He could feel the presence of something evil, something that wanted to harm him. Lights started to flicker.

Suddenly, a shadowy figure emerged from the darkness, its eyes glowing with a sinister light. The boy's blood ran cold as he recognized the figure. It was the horse, the harbinger of doom.

The boy, paralyzed with fear, stepped backward. But as he did, the ground that disappeared before beneath him gave way, and he fell into a dark room. The darkness enveloped him, and he was alone, a solitary figure in a world of shadows.

The room was silent, except for the sound of his own labored breathing. He tried to see, but the darkness was impenetrable. He reached out, his hands groping in the darkness, but he could touch nothing.

He was lost, alone, and afraid. He didn't know where he was or what was going to happen to him. All he knew was that he had to find a way out, to escape the clutches of darkness.

He took a deep breath and began to move forward, his hands outstretched, feeling his way through the darkness. He stumbled and fell, but he kept moving, driven by a desperate desire to survive.Meanwhile, on the chessboard, the white king stood firm, a last sign of hope in the grim surroundings. But as the knight advanced, something shifted. The king, once full of strength, seemed to lose his grip on the game. In one sudden move, he was knocked over, disappearing into the thick shadows of the room. The light of hope that had been there just moments ago was now gone, replaced by an overwhelming darkness.

CHAPTER TWELVE

THE RED PRISON

Here's another room,

The room felt cold, almost hostile. It was simple, plain, with bare brick walls that looked rough and unpainted. Nothing fancy. Just a small bulb hanging from the ceiling, casting shadows on the cracked floor. The light flickered a little, the only source of illumination in the otherwise dark space. The silence in the room was heavy, almost suffocating. The only noise was the low hum of the light and the sound of her own breathing.

She was trapped.

A young woman, dressed in a bright red chudidar, sat in the center of the room. Her wide, frightened eyes darted from corner to corner, searching for anything that could help her escape. But it was no use. There was no way out. The walls were solid, and the only opening—a door—was nowhere to be found. She reached out to touch the wall, but it was as cold and unforgiving as everything else in the room.

Her heart raced, her breaths shallow and quick. She felt like she was losing control, like the walls were closing in on her with every passing second. The ticking of the old clock was the only thing that reminded her of time. Each tick felt like it was echoing in her skull, counting down to something unknown.

She stood up, trying to shake off the fear. Maybe there was something she missed—some hidden latch, a crack in the wall she hadn't noticed. She ran her hands along the rough surface of the brick, feeling for anything that could help her escape. But there was nothing. No hidden door, no secret passage. It was just a small, empty room.

The ticking of the clock grew louder in her ears as her hope began to fade. She sank back down to the floor, her legs folding beneath her. She hugged her knees to her chest, tears welling up in her eyes. The reality of it all hit her like a punch to the gut. She was trapped. Completely and utterly trapped.

With each passing minute, the room felt more and more like a prison. The walls seemed to close in tighter, and the air felt thicker, harder to breathe. She tried to focus, to calm her racing thoughts. But it was impossible. The silence, the loneliness, the ticking clock—it all mixed together into a storm of panic in her chest.

Why had she been put here? Who did this to her? What did they want? She tried to force her mind to think logically, to figure out a way out, but the fear had taken over. She felt small, helpless, and alone.

The minutes turned to hours, or maybe it was just her mind playing tricks on her. It felt like time had stopped, or maybe it was moving too fast. Either way, it didn't matter. She was still here, still trapped in this cold, empty room with no way out.

She wiped her face, the tears still flowing. The fear was relentless, gnawing at her, pulling her deeper into despair. There had to be a way out. There had to be something she missed. But the walls were solid, and the clock continued to tick.

She closed her eyes, trying to think of something—anything—that could give her hope. She remembered the world outside, the noise, the people, the life she once knew. It felt like a distant dream now, like it never really existed. Was she ever going to leave this place? Was anyone coming for her?

The room offered no answers, only more questions. The ticking clock was a constant reminder that time was slipping away, and she was no closer to finding an escape. She could feel the panic rising again, the tightness in her chest growing. She wanted to scream, to bang on the walls, to demand answers. But all she could do was sit there, trapped in the silence.

With a shaky breath, she wiped her face again. She was done crying. She couldn't afford to waste any more time on fear. She had to think, had to find a way out. She stood up once more, determination beginning to replace the hopelessness. Her hands ran over the walls again, this time with more purpose. She wasn't going to stop until she found something—anything—that could lead her to freedom.The clock continued to tick, but now it felt different. It wasn't just a reminder of time. It was a challenge. She had no idea how long she had been there or how long she would be stuck, but she knew one thing for sure—she wasn't going to give up without a fight.

CHAPTER THIRTEEN

THE FLAME OF DESPAIR

The darkness felt heavy in the room where the boy is. It pressed against him, thick and suffocating, like it was trying to swallow him whole. The boy's heart raced as he stumbled forward. He couldn't see a thing. All he could feel was the emptiness around him, the cold, and the weight of the dark that seemed to be everywhere.

He tried to stay calm. Panic wouldn't help. But it was hard, very hard.

His hands reached out, desperate to find something—anything—that could help. His fingers brushed against something cold. A table. He grabbed it, using it to steady himself.

On the table, there was something old. An oil lamp. It was small, simple, and not very special at first glance. But to him, in that moment, it was everything. The only thing that could push away the darkness.

But it was useless without a flame. The lamp was just a sad, cold object in the dark. He needed to light it, but how?

His heart sank. It was as if the weight of the world rested on this tiny lamp. If only he could light it. If only he had a match, a spark of fire. He knew that once the lamp was lit, the darkness would go away. But right now, it felt impossible.

His mind raced as he tried to think. "Where can I find a match? There has to be one somewhere."

The boy knew he couldn't give up. He had to try. He fumbled around the table, opening drawers and feeling through the dark. He had to find a match. He had no choice. He couldn't stay in this dark forever.

His hands searched desperately. He opened every drawer. There was nothing. His panic was rising, but he forced himself to take deep breaths. He wouldn't give up. Not now.

Then, he felt it—a tiny latch on the back of the table. His heart skipped. Could it be?

He pulled it open. Inside, there was a small, hidden compartment. He reached in, fingers trembling. What was inside?

A small, wooden box. His breath caught in his throat. Could this be it? Could this box hold what he needed to light the lamp?

He opened the box slowly, his heart racing. Inside, two matches. Just two. But that was all he needed.

He stared at the matches for a moment, a surge of hope flooding through him. This was it. The darkness would end now.

But then, a thought hit him. What if the matches didn't work? What if they were too old, too weak?

No. He couldn't think like that.

He took a match from the box and carefully struck it against the side. Nothing. He tried again. Still nothing. His fingers were trembling, his breath coming faster as panic began to rise.

He tried one more time, his heart pounding in his chest. This time, the match lit.

A tiny flame flickered at the tip. He held his breath, watching it carefully. The match didn't burn out. The flame stayed, and the darkness around him seemed to pull back just a little bit.

The boy's heart soared with relief.

The boy stood there, staring at the flame. The weight was gone. The silence, the fear—it was all gone. In that moment, he knew one thing for sure: sometimes, all it takes is a spark to light up the world.

The room was bathed in a dim, flickering light, barely illuminating the shadowy corners.

The sound of a ticking clock filled the room, steady and unyielding. It was as if the clock itself was watching him, waiting for something to happen. Each tick seemed louder than the last, growing closer to midnight. The boy could feel the tension in the air, thick with something he couldn't name.

His heart raced as he watched the second hand of the clock move closer to twelve. He had a strange feeling, a sense that something bad was coming. He glanced back at the clock.

Tick... tick... tick...

Then, the clock struck twelve.

Dong... dong... dong...

The sound of the chimes echoed in the room, each one louder and more unsettling than the last. The boy's heart skipped a beat. It wasn't just the sound that scared him; it was the cold, creeping feeling in his chest. Something wasn't right.

The air in the room felt colder, heavier. He couldn't explain why, but he felt trapped. The chimes seemed to reach deep inside him, pulling out a fear he couldn't shake. He swallowed hard, his throat dry.

The boy's eyes darted around, searching for anything that could help.

The dim light flickering in his hands felt like his only source of hope in this dark room.

He stepped forward slowly, holding the lamp in front of him. The shadows in the room seemed to stretch and move, like they had a life of their own. Every step he took felt like a step deeper into the unknown.

There had to be an escape from this nightmare. But when he looked around, he realized something terrible—he was trapped. The room was small, with bare walls and no doors or windows. It was like a cage made from his own fear.

He turned in circles, scanning every corner. His mind raced as he searched for an escape, but there was nothing. Despair crept in, making his legs weak. Was there no way out?

Just as he was about to give up, something caught his eye. On a small table, an old book lay open. Its leather cover was worn, and the pages were yellowed with age. Curious, he walked over and picked it up.

The book felt heavy in his hands, like it was holding a secret. As he stared at the open pages, he saw strange symbols and words that didn't make sense to him. But then, something stood out. A map.

The map was strange. It wasn't just a normal map. It was filled with tiny letters and symbols, all crammed together in a way that made it hard to understand. Each symbol seemed to be trying to tell him something, but the boy couldn't quite figure out what it meant. The boy studied it closely, his mind working quickly. Could this map show him how to escape?

He leaned closer, squinting at the symbols. There was a message hidden in there, he was sure of it. But it was like a puzzle, each symbol a clue to something bigger. He could almost feel that the answer was within reach, but he wasn't sure how to unlock it.

He leaned in, squinting at the map. His heart beat faster as he realized something. This might be the key. The only question was—could he figure it out before time ran out?

The boy bent closer to the map in the book, trying to make sense of it. His mind raced, trying to figure out the twists and turns of the lines. He felt like he was on the verge of solving the puzzle, of finding his escape. But just as his fingers traced the path on the map, something went horribly wrong.

The oil lamp in his hand, which he had been holding to light his way, suddenly tilted. It was as if it had a life of its own. The flame caught the edge of the book, and within seconds, the pages were ablaze.

He froze for a moment, watching in horror as the fire spread, eating up the map, the pages, and everything that he had hoped would lead him out of the room.

The boy's heart hammered in his chest. He quickly tried to blow out the flames, but it was too late. The fire had already taken hold of the book, and within moments, the once-crisp pages were turning to ash. The smell of burning paper filled the air. It was thick, heavy, and acrid. The boy coughed, his eyes stinging from the smoke.

Panic rose inside him. The map—the only thing that had seemed to offer a way out—was gone. The boy felt his chest tighten. He had been so close. So close to finding a way to escape this room, and now it was all lost in the flames.

As the fire slowly died down, the boy sat back, defeated. The room was filled with smoke, the air thick with the remains of the burning book. His hands trembled as he reached for the book again, now completely charred. The map was gone. The pages, once filled with hope, were now nothing but blank sheets, empty and useless.

He held the book in his hands, staring at the blackened pages. A deep sense of disappointment settled in his chest. He had been so sure that the map would show him the way out. But now, there was nothing. The path to freedom, the only chance he had, had vanished in the smoke.

He closed the book with a heavy heart. A feeling of hopelessness washed over him. He was alone, trapped in a room full of shadows, with no way to escape. It felt like the darkness was closing in on him, and there was nothing he could do to stop it.

The boy sank to the ground, his mind blank.

CHAPTER FOURTEEN

THE DICE OF FATE

Meanwhile, in the other room, the girl, frustrated and desperate, paced back and forth. She had searched every inch of the room, but there was no sign of a way out. As soon as the book in the boy's room turned to ashes, a brick in here fell from the ceiling, revealing a small, hidden compartment. Inside the compartment, she found a single, six-sided die.

Curiosity peaked, she picked up the die and examined it. It was an ordinary die, nothing special. But as she held it in her hand, a strange feeling washed over her. She tossed the die onto the floor, watching as it rolled and tumbled. It came to a stop, revealing a number five facing up.

A shiver ran down her spine. What did the number five mean? Was it a clue, a puzzle, or something more sinister? She stared at the die, her mind racing.

On the otherside, the boy, his mind racing, desperately searching for a solution. He knew he couldn't stay in this dark, confined space forever. As he scanned the room, his gaze fell upon the old, leather-bound book. A strange sensation washed over him, a feeling of familiarity.

The book, as if beckoning him, slowly opened its pages. One by one, the pages turned, revealing a hidden message.

Finally, the book settled on page five, a chilling image emerging from the darkness.

A drawing, crude yet haunting, depicted a young girl, her figure half-hidden by a red shawl. Her eyes, wide with fear, seemed to pierce through the paper.

The girl in the drawing was clinging to the shawl, her grip tight.

The boy's heart pounded in his chest as he stared at the drawing. A wave of recognition washed over him. The girl in the drawing bore a striking resemblance to his friend, the one he had lost.

A sense of urgency gripped the boy. He had to find her, to save her. He turned the pages of the book, hoping to find more clues, more answers. But the pages remained blank, a void.

As he stared at the drawing, a chilling realization dawned upon him. The girl in the drawing was in danger, perhaps even in the same predicament as him. He had to find her, to rescue her. But how? The answer, he knew, lay within the pages of the book.

In the room where the girl is, at first, it felt impossible. The bricks seemed solid, unmovable. But then, one of them shifted slightly. Encouraged, she tugged harder, her hands trembling but determined. Slowly, one brick came loose. Then another. And another.

After what felt like forever, she had managed to remove five bricks. There it was—a small opening. She could feel a faint breeze coming through, a promise of the world outside. For a second, hope flickered in her chest. Maybe this was it. Maybe she could escape.

But then she decided to try her luck, thinking she could make the hole bigger. She reached for the next brick, but something strange happened. It wouldn't budge. No matter how hard she tried, the brick stayed in place.

Confused, she tried the other bricks around it. Nothing. It was like the wall had suddenly decided it wasn't going to help her anymore. She pushed, pulled, hit the wall with her fists, but it didn't work.

Maybe its the dice.

She looked at the dice in her hand, her fingers trembling slightly. Taking a deep breath, she threw it across the floor. The dice tumbled, spinning wildly before finally landing on a six.

Her heart leaped. A six! Relief washed over her. Maybe luck was finally on her side. A smile broke out on her face as she turned to the wall, ready to remove more bricks.

She crouched down and reached for the next brick, gripping it tightly and pulling with all her strength. But it wouldn't move. She frowned, trying another one. Still no luck.

Her smile faltered as she tried again, harder this time. Nothing. The bricks didn't even shift. It was like the wall had suddenly become indestructible.

She peered through the opening, her eyes scanning the darkness beyond. She could make out the faint outline of another room, a glimmer of hope in the darkness. With renewed determination, she tied her red shawl to the metal grill outside the brick hole, creating a makeshift rope.

The girl carefully climbed out of the brick hole, her grip tightening on the shawl. The wind whipped at her, threatening to pull her from the precarious perch. She closed her eyes, taking a deep breath. With a leap of faith, she swung down, the shawl cutting through the air.

As she descended, the girl couldn't shake the feeling that she was being watched. She glanced up at the window, and for a brief moment, she thought she saw a figure peering out at her. But as quickly as it appeared, the figure vanished, leaving her alone with her thoughts.

Meanwhile, in the other room, the boy continued to study the drawing. The girl in the drawing, with her desperate plea for help, mirrored his own situation. He knew he had to find a way to help her, to rescue her from the clutches of darkness. But how? The answer, he believed, lay within the pages of the book.

CHAPTER FIFTEEN

FALLING INTO THE GAME

The boy stared at the drawing, his heart racing. The more he studied it, the more details stood out—details that seemed important. The floor of the room, illustrated in the drawing, looked like a something he stood before. It wasn't just the pattern; it was the way the tiles were arranged, each square in perfect alignment. A shiver ran down his spine. Was this a clue? A hint to get out of this strange, locked room?

He had to act fast. His mind raced as he looked for anything that could explain the drawing. The floor, the girl, the way everything fit together—was it all connected? He couldn't be sure, but it felt like something bigger than him was at play.

With newfound determination, he rushed to the spot where he had fallen. This time, his gaze went upwards. And there she was—the girl from the drawing. Her face was pale, her eyes wide with fear, clinging to a red shawl that was barely holding her.

"Shifali!" he shouted, his voice echoing. But the silence swallowed his words. The room remained dead quiet. As his shout faded, the ceiling began to change. A heavy, metallic door slowly slid into place, closing off the view of the girl.

His stomach twisted in fear. Was she trapped, like him?

Shifali's grip on the rope was faltering. The frayed edges of the shawl she clung to seemed to be unraveling with every passing second. The wind howled, pulling at her, threatening to send her falling into the unknown. Her fingers were slipping. She could feel the cold, sharp edges of the shawl cutting into her skin as her strength faded.

In that moment, she let go.

The world spun as she fell, a rush of wind filling her ears. She braced herself for impact, expecting to crash hard onto the ground. But when she landed, it wasn't what she had imagined.

Her body didn't hit the cold, hard floor with a thud. Instead, it was softer. It was as if she had fallen onto something strange—something that didn't belong. She blinked, trying to focus.

She felt dizzy, disoriented, like she had entered a different realm. And then, a single name slipped from her lips, barely a whisper. She was calling him.

"Iniyan..."

Her voice seemed to vanish into the vastness of the room. But somehow, the name echoed back to her. The room around her flickered, and she could see faint lights glowing in the distance. The shadows seemed to shift as if the room itself were alive.

Slowly, her vision cleared, and she realized she was lying on a....

A massive chessboard.

The black and white squares stretched endlessly in all directions. Her chest tightened as she looked around, unable to make sense of her surroundings. She had fallen into a game, into a world that didn't feel real.

She tried to move, but everything was strange. She stood, her knees trembling as she adjusted to the uneven surface. The chessboard beneath her feet felt alive, as though every square beneath her carried some weight, some importance.

Meanwhile, across the room in the mysterious, dark space, the white queen had replaced the position of the white king, and now it was the queen's turn. The chessboard was alive in its own way, each piece representing more than just an object. Each piece was connected to something. Someone.

And on the other side, Shifali took the position of the Queen. She bacame a part of the game. The chess piece movements weren't random. They were controlled. Every time she shifted or moved, so did the queen.

It was as if the girl and the queen were one and the same. Shifali, still lying on the board, had no idea of the connection. She had no idea that the queen on the chessboard in the room was her. And she had no idea that her every move mirrored the queen's—without her knowledge, the girl was playing a game of life and death. The girl was the queen, the queen was her.

CHAPTER SIXTEEN

The Queen's Entry

The boy, desperate to find a way to rescue Shifali, turned his attention back to the book. He flipped through the pages, hoping to find a clue, a hint, a way out. But the pages were blank, except for the one with the drawing.

Disappointment washed over him. The book, once a beacon of hope, had become a dead end. He closed the book, his heart heavy with despair. He was trapped, a prisoner in a world of darkness.

On the other side,

The room the girl is there was dark, the only source of light a dim, flickering lamp hanging on top of her. The air was still and silent, the only sound the ticking of a clock. She sat up, her heart pounding.

Lights started flickering. She looked around, her eyes scanning the room, but there was nothing she could make out. The checked floor seemed to glow faintly in the strange dim light, but beyond that, everything else was swallowed in darkness. The only thing clearly visible was the chessboard beneath her.

The walls were bare, the floor cold and hard.

She tried to stand up, but her legs were weak, unsteady. Her body felt heavy, like it didn't belong to her. The place is completely quiet.

As she takes a step forward, she could sense something that's standing right before her.

She forced herself to take a step forward, but as soon as she did, a chill ran through her. It felt like something was standing right in front of her, waiting.

Her breath caught in her throat. She turned slowly, and there it was. A black horse. It stood still in the middle of the room, its eyes glowing with a strange, almost sinister light. The sight of it sent a wave of fear through her.

The horse neighed, the sound sharp and unsettling. It reared up on its hind legs, its hooves pounding against the floor. The sound echoed in her ears, each thundering step making her heart race faster.

The girl froze, her body shaking. Her instincts screamed at her to run, but she couldn't move. She closed her eyes, bracing herself for what she knew was coming. She had no idea what this was, but she could feel it—whatever it was, it meant danger.

A scream rose in her chest, but before it could escape her lips, something strange happened. The scream was swallowed by the silence, as if the very air around her had absorbed it.

When she opened her eyes, the horse was gone. Vanished, like it had never been there. The room was empty again, the silence even more oppressive than before. The only thing left was the faintly glowing floor beneath her, and the shadows creeping in from every corner.

Meanwhile, on the chessboard in the mysterious room, the queen stood tall, a symbol of power and strength. Her movements were swift and decisive, and with a single push, she had kicked the knight off the board. The knight, once a formidable opponent, had been defeated. The game, though quiet and still, felt alive in its own way.

Yes, she was connected to the queen on the chessboard, placed in that mysterious room.

And now, in the very spot where the white king had once stood, isolated and defeated, the white queen took her place on the chessboard in the mysterious room. The king's fall had left a void, a moment of weakness that now seemed to transform into something powerful. The queen, once just a piece among many, now commanded the board with an authority that resonated through the stillness of the room. It was as though the game had shifted entirely, and with it, her destiny.

CHAPTER SEVENTEEN

THE TICKING CLOCK

Meanwhile, in another realm, the boy was growing increasingly anxious. As soon as the Queen kicked off the Knight in the mysterious room, the timer suddenly started ticking, its seconds growing shorter.

He has 10 minutes but he had no idea why the clock was ticking, or what it was counting down to. A sense of dread washed over him as he realized that time was running out.

He turned his attention back to the book, hoping to find a clue, a hint, a way to escape. But the book remained silent, its pages offering no answers. Frustration and fear gnawed at him. He paced the room, his mind racing.

He bit his nails, his mind racing. Why was the clock ticking? What was it counting down to?

As he pondered this question, he suddenly glanced at his wristwatch. A chill ran down his spine. The watch was ticking too, but it was ticking on the same area. It didn't move further.

Intrigued, the boy turned the watch, rotating the hands counterclockwise. As he did so, a strange sensation washed over him. He felt as if he was reliving a moment, a memory. He saw himself, a few minutes ago, walking, analysing the book, shouting Shifali, lost in thought.

He realized that the watch was not just a timepiece; it was a tool, a device that could manipulate time.

Perhaps the clock was not just a timer, but a portal to the past. A desperate hope ignited within him.

But as the time on the watch dwindled, so too did his ability to see into the past. The images became blurry, then faded into nothingness. He was left with a fleeting glimpse of the past, a tantalizing glimpse of what could have been.

The boy realized that he could only rewind time for a limited period and it is linked with the timer. He had to use this power wisely, to make every moment count.

The boy fiddled nervously with the dial of his wristwatch, his fingers moving swiftly as he rewound time. He wasn't thinking about the present anymore—his mind was set on getting back to the moment he was studying the map. That's where he needed to be. The room around him seemed to hum faintly, the air growing thicker as the seconds ticked backward on his watch.

As he turned the dial, an idea struck him. What if I could just pause it?

The thought lit a spark of curiosity. For a brief moment, he stopped rewinding and pressed down on the watch's face, as if willing it to freeze time altogether. His breath caught, and he waited.

Nothing.

The seconds continued to slip through his grasp, relentless and unyielding. The watch refused to pause, no matter how hard he tried. He gritted his teeth, frustration bubbling up inside him.

A glance at the watch made his heart sink. Only eight minutes remained. Eight precious minutes he could rewind. That was all the time he had to work with.

He clenched his jaw, refocusing. No time to waste now. He spun the dial again, faster this time, watching as the clock pulled him back toward the critical moment—the moment he'd been analyzing the map.

This has to work, he thought, determination burning in his chest. It has to.

As he turned back the dial one last time, the book— the one he had been poring over before lay open before him.

The map was there.

He focused his attention on the map, the cryptic message that held the key to his escape. He knew that he had to decipher the map quickly, before time ran out.

But something about it felt different this time. The lines seemed sharper, the symbols almost alive, pulsating faintly as though aware of his presence.

But this time, strangely though the book got lit by the lamp again like before, the map in the book didn't disappear.

His breath quickened. This can't be real. Can it?

He leaned closer, the ticking of his watch growing louder in his ears. It was a cruel reminder—time was still slipping away. And the map... the map might vanish once the hands of the watch began to move forward again.

No, he thought, urgency coursing through him. I can't let this moment slip away.

As he worked, the clock ticked away, each second bringing him closer to the end. He knew that he had to hurry, that he had to find the solution before it was too late.

With renewed determination, he studied the map, his eyes scanning the intricate details. He noticed a pattern, a sequence of symbols that seemed to form a code. He began to decipher the code, his mind racing.

He knew that he had to hurry, that he had to find the solution before it was too late.

Finally, after what felt like an eternity, he cracked the code. The map revealed a hidden passage, a secret door.

A rush of adrenaline flooded his veins. His heart raced as he rushed towards the book, determined to study the map again, to commit it to memory. But just as he reached out to grasp the fragile pages once more, something unexpected happened.

FWOOSH!

The book in his hand burst into flames.

The fire spread rapidly, engulfing the room. The boy, caught off guard, stumbled backward.

In the chaos, the boy remembered the cryptic symbols on the map. He realized that the symbols might hold the key to solving the puzzle. He grabbed the lamp from the fire and began to examine the walls of the room. His hands trembled slightly, but he steadied them as he moved toward the spot the map had indicated.

As he moved the lamp across the walls, he noticed something strange. In certain areas, the paint on the wall seemed to darken, revealing hidden words when the flame in the lamp neared it. The words were faint, almost invisible, but with the help of the lamp, he was able to decipher them.

The words formed a sequence, a riddle. The boy studied the sequence, his mind racing. He realized that they were clues, something to his escape.

He had seen enough strange things that day to last a lifetime. But nothing prepared him for what he was about to find behind that wall.

He stood there, staring at the stone wall in front of him. The door was massive, with invisible letters that darkened as the flame in the lamp neared it. There was no handle, no keyhole—just an inscription that made his stomach twist:

"Bring me to life, and I'll grant you sight.
In my glow, the path ignites."

He read it again, just to make sure he hadn't imagined it. What the hell did that even mean? The only thing he knew for sure was that if he didn't do something, he'd be stuck in this creepy place forever.

He looked around, his eyes scanning the dimly lit room. His pulse was racing—something was wrong. The walls felt too close, like they were closing in on him. And then, he saw it. A small indentation at the bottom of the wall. It was blackened, like something had burned there long ago.

Without thinking, he grabbed a match from his pocket and lit it. He wasn't sure why—he had just a match, but something told him that if he didn't light it, he'd never know what was on the other side.

Holding the flame to the indentation, he waited for something to happen. And sure enough, the second the fire touched the blackened surface, the wall gave a low groan, like it was waking up from a long sleep. The flames from the match flickered, casting weird shadows on the walls.

As the flames consumed the walls, a secret door appeared. The boy, filled with hope, stepped through the door, ready to face whatever challenges lay ahead. He knew that the journey had just begun, and that the ultimate prize, the freedom of Shifali, was within reach.

CHAPTER EIGHTEEN

THE SILENT QUEEN

He opened the door and stepped inside.

The room beyond was pitch black. He could barely make out the shape of the walls. But then something caught his eye—something in the darkness.

There was a glass pane embedded in the wall, and through it, he saw... something.

He squinted, his heart starting to race. The glass wasn't completely clear—it shimmered faintly, like it was somehow alive, reacting to the light. And then he saw it—

Shifali.

She was on a massive chessboard, in the place of the white queen. The entire room looked like a giant chess set. This wasn't just a game. The black pieces—knights, rooks, and pawns—loomed over her, their surfaces dark and glossy, almost like polished stone. But there was no mistaking it. Shifali was right there.

Her face was emotionless, almost blank. Her eyes were fixed on nothing, like she wasn't even aware he was watching her.

"Shifali!" he whispered, his voice cracking.

He pressed his hand against the glass. The chill of it sent a shiver up his spine. There was no response from her, no movement. She was just... there.

The room behind the glass felt unnaturally quiet, like everything had been frozen in time. But something was off. The chess pieces—those black pawns—they were all turned towards her. Not in a normal way. More like they were watching her. Waiting.

"Shifali!" he tried again, this time louder.

Nothing. Not a flicker, not a single movement.

He stepped back from the glass, trying to figure out what was going on. Was this some kind of sick joke? Was this some messed-up game?

But then, just as he was about to turn away, he heard a sound.

It was a scraping sound. Something behind him.

He whipped around, his heart leaping into his throat. The hallway he had just walked through was as dark as ever, but there was a strange feeling in the air. The air felt... wrong. Thick. Like something was lurking in the shadows, waiting to pounce.

"Okay, calm down," he told himself, trying to steady his breathing.

But the scraping continued. Closer now.

He stepped back, his feet suddenly heavy. He couldn't explain it, but he felt like he wasn't alone anymore. Like something was watching him—no, waiting for him to make the next move.

He glanced at the door behind him. The one he had just opened. Was it possible that whatever was in the other room had been waiting for him all along? Waiting for him to open the door?

He didn't want to believe it, but he knew he had no choice but to move forward. He couldn't leave Shifali like that. He had to find out what was going on.

He glanced one last time at the glass. She was still sitting there, unmoving. The black pieces, still watching her.

He took a deep breath, bracing himself for whatever came next.

But as he turned toward the hallway again, he realized something else. The shadows weren't just shadows. They were moving. The black pawns—they weren't just watching Shifali. They were watching him.

And then, he heard it.

A whisper, so soft he almost missed it.

"You shouldn't have come."

The hairs on the back of his neck stood up. His heart slammed against his ribcage. He wasn't alone.

He wasn't sure if he was in a nightmare. He wasn't even sure if he was still in the real world.

But he knew one thing.

He had to get Shifali out of there.

And if he didn't, he might be trapped in that dark room forever.

CHAPTER NINETEEN

THE GAME'S EDGE

He backed away from the glass, his mind racing. There was something terribly wrong about this. It was like a one-sided mirror—he could see Shifali clearly, but she couldn't hear him. She didn't even seem to acknowledge his presence.

"Shifali!" He shouted again, his voice cracking, but it was as if the room was swallowing his words. She remained motionless, trapped in that strange, lifeless state. The glass between them felt like an impenetrable barrier, mocking him with its smooth, silent surface.

His mind raced—there has to be a way to break through. To reach her.

He scanned the room, desperately searching for something, anything, that could help him. His hands shook as he moved along the walls, his fingers brushing against the cold stone and the heavy wooden beams. There was nothing—no tools, no sharp objects. Just the same cold emptiness.

He turned back to the glass, his face flushed with frustration. "Shifali, please, look at me!" But still, there was no response.

What the hell was this place?

Then, it hit him. Maybe it wasn't about shouting. Maybe he needed to break the glass. He looked at his hands. Bare. Useless. But what choice did he have?

He balled up his fists and slammed them against the glass. The sound was deafening, like a thunderclap echoing through the room. But the glass didn't crack. It barely even shuddered.

His frustration turned to panic. He hit the glass again—harder this time. It made a dull, hollow sound, but nothing else. He could feel his knuckles beginning to sting, the pain intensifying with each strike, but still, the glass held firm.

"Come on! Come on!" he muttered under his breath, desperation creeping in.

Then, just as he was about to strike again, something strange happened.

The glass seemed to ripple. A faint vibration ran through it. He froze. He had seen it—the surface of the glass was changing, distorting slightly, almost like it was alive.

His heart hammered in his chest. Maybe it was finally weakening. Maybe, just maybe, he could break through to her.

He slammed his fist against it one more time, harder, with every ounce of strength he had left. The glass cracked—just a little at first. A thin spider-web of fractures appeared, spreading out from the point of impact.

He felt a rush of hope.

But then, as his hand touched the broken surface, something strange happened.

A sharp, cold pull.

It was like an invisible force, grabbing hold of him, dragging him away from the glass. He tried to fight it, to dig his feet into the floor, but the force was too strong.

"No!" he shouted, panic rising.

His fingers slipped from the broken edge of the glass, and he stumbled backward. The pull was relentless, like something was reaching out from the other side, urging him to leave.

"Go away".

The words weren't spoken. They didn't need to be. It was as if the air itself was whispering to him, warning him to step back.

But he couldn't stop. He had to get to her. He couldn't just let her stay trapped in that hellish place.

He took a deep breath and ran towards the glass again, slamming his body against it, his shoulder digging into the cool surface. The impact sent a shockwave through him, but the glass didn't crack further. Instead, the force pulling him away intensified, now dragging at his chest, his legs, his arms. It was as if the entire room was conspiring to push him out.

And then, another whisper.

"Go away."

This time, it was louder—stronger. He could feel it, pressing into his mind. It wasn't just a warning; it was a command.

His body froze. The air around him thickened. He felt himself getting weaker, like whatever was pulling him away was draining his strength. He tried to push forward again, but it was futile. He couldn't fight it.

The glass stopped vibrating. The cracks that had appeared on the surface slowly started to seal up, as though the glass was healing itself.

He could barely hold his eyes open now, his mind clouded by the invisible force.

He staggered back, breathless, his hands pressed against his sides. The pull was gone, but so was his resolve. The glass was whole again, solid, impenetrable.

He stood there, helpless, staring at the woman he couldn't reach. The pieces of the chessboard loomed around her, those dark pawns still standing guard, as if they were waiting for the next move.

He could do nothing. And it felt like everything was slipping away.

He was standing there, eyes glued to the glass, when something made him pause.

Shifali—Shifali was moving.

For the first time, her lips trembled. Her hands, which had been resting lifelessly on her lap, twitched. Her fingers brushed against the cool surface of the chessboard, as if trying to make a move.

A sliver of hope flickered inside him. She was still in there. She could still be saved.

But that hope was quickly swallowed by the growing dread that he couldn't reach her. Not through the glass. Not with his voice.

Desperation clawed at his chest, the pull of the unseen force still heavy on his soul. He turned away from the glass, instinctively searching the room around him.

The lamp. He needed the lamp.

His eyes found it almost immediately, sitting in the corner where he had left it. He dashed to it, snatching it up with shaking hands. The heavy base of the lamp felt solid in his grip. This was it. This was his chance.

He turned back toward the glass, swinging the lamp with all his strength. The lamp collided with the mirror-like surface with a resounding crash. A spiderweb of cracks ran through the glass, but it didn't break. The mirror resisted, as if it had its own will, its own purpose.

He swung again, harder this time, his whole body straining with the effort. It has to break. It just has to.

The glass groaned under the pressure, a low, sickening sound that made his stomach twist. Then, with one final, bone-jarring hit, the glass shattered.

For a split second, he thought he'd done it—he'd finally done it.

But as the shards of glass tumbled to the ground, something worse happened. The entire room seemed to collapse in on itself. The scene beyond—the chessboard, Shifali, the dark black pawns—vanished in a swirling cloud of smoke and dust.

He staggered back, his heart pounding in his chest, his vision blurry from the chaos.

Where was Shifali? Where was the chessboard?

The room—the entire room—was gone. There was nothing left but a solid black wall, as if the glass had never been there at all.

And then, just as the last remnants of smoke swirled into the air, a voice boomed from the darkness.

"You did the biggest mistake."

The words echoed around him, coming from every direction, as if the very air was speaking to him.

Before he could even react, a powerful force seized his legs. It felt like invisible hands were grabbing at his ankles, pulling him into the blackness.

"No!" he shouted, but his voice was drowned by the sudden pressure. His feet left the ground, and he was yanked backward, stumbling and helpless, into another room.

The walls were dark and cold, but this room was different. It wasn't just the atmosphere—it was the presence inside.

There were giant white chess pieces all around him, massive and imposing. Pawns, rooks, knights, all locked inside transparent cages, their oversized forms looming like silent giants in the shadows.

He couldn't understand what he was seeing. The pieces were so large, they made him feel tiny in comparison. Some of them had cracks running through their smooth surfaces, as though they were damaged from something—or someone—trying to break out.

"What is this place?" he whispered, the words barely escaping his lips.

But there was no answer.

He stepped forward, his mind reeling. The door behind him slammed shut with a deafening noise, the sound vibrating through the room. It felt like he was trapped now—really trapped, with no way out.

And then, the floor beneath him shifted. He felt the ground rumble, the room itself alive with energy.

The chess pieces began to move. Slowly at first. The giant pawns stirred, their large forms creaking with a life of their own.

A cold chill ran down his spine. What did this mean? Why were the pieces moving?

The energy in the room was building, vibrating with an intensity he couldn't explain. It was like the air was charged with something... something alive.

He turned in every direction, his eyes scanning the room for an escape. But the walls were solid. The cages around the chess pieces? Inescapable.

And then, he heard it.

A deep, booming voice—the same one that had spoken to him before.

"You have entered the realm of the game. And now, you are one of its pieces."

CHAPTER TWENTY

THE KING'S COMMAND

His heart was racing in his chest as he scrambled through the room, trying to avoid the giant chess pieces that were now moving towards him. The massive white pawns and rooks groaned as they shifted across the floor, their enormous shapes casting long, dark shadows on the cold, polished surface. The knights—no, the horses—moved slowly, their heavy hooves echoing throughout the room with every step. The sound was like thunder, each stomp a reminder of how dangerous this place was.

In the chaos, one thought kept repeating itself in his mind—Where can I go? What can I do?

He kept his head low, darting between the chess pieces, doing his best to stay hidden. But then, something strange caught his attention. It wasn't just the pieces that were moving. The white pieces—they weren't just playing the game. It was as if they were trapped in it. Their faces, once lifeless and mechanical, now looked... bitter. Almost as if they were aware of their fate, stuck in these roles and unable to escape. They looked tired, worn out, and filled with anger.

As he turned to make his next move, he realized something worse—their eyes were on him.

At first, he thought it was just his imagination, some trick of the mind. But then it became clear. The white chess pieces were staring at him, watching him with purpose. It wasn't just coincidence. They saw him as an enemy. The feeling was unmistakable—they thought he was here to destroy them, to end their existence.

The giant horses stopped moving for a moment. Their eyes locked onto him, their heads rearing up in the air. The pawns and rooks turned, almost in unison, their movements deliberate, as if they had been waiting for this moment. The room felt heavier, like a trap slowly closing around him. It was as if they had known all along that someone would come to challenge them. And now, it was his turn.

The room was eerily silent, but the walls weren't. Everywhere he looked, he saw the faces of people who had been stuck in this game. Carvings were etched into the walls, images of people—no, souls—trapped forever in the game. Their faces were twisted in pain, their eyes wide with fear. It was like they were begging him to stop, to not get caught in whatever was happening. But it was too late for them. They had been here for too long.

He looked around desperately, scanning for a way out. And then, at the far end of the room, he saw it—a massive statue, towering over everything else. His only chance.

Without thinking, he bolted towards it. The pounding of the horses' hooves grew louder, the other chess pieces closing in. He ran faster, his heart in his throat, but the tension in the air was unbearable. His breath was coming in ragged gasps, his legs burning with each step, but he didn't stop. The statue—he had to reach it.

Just as he was almost there, one of the giant horses turned its head and saw him. Its eyes locked onto his, and the terror of being caught flashed through him. He dove behind the statue, hoping it would shield him. His body pressed against the cold, smooth marble, trying to make himself as small as possible. He held his breath, praying that the chess pieces wouldn't notice him hiding there.

For a moment, there was nothing. The horses stopped moving. The pawns and rooks froze. Everything seemed to hold its breath, waiting. He didn't dare move, didn't dare make a sound. He stayed pressed against the statue, his heart pounding so loudly he was sure they could hear it. He let out a quiet sigh of relief.

But then, as he slowly peered around the statue's base, he realized something that made his blood run cold.

The statue he was hiding behind wasn't just any piece.

It was the White King.

Iniyan's heart raced as he hid behind the towering White King statue, trying to stay as still as possible. The room was alive with tension, the chess pieces moving with purpose, each one casting long shadows across the cold floor. His mind raced, trying to make sense of what was happening.

It was then that his eyes were drawn to something on the statue's crown—the jewel. A single, vibrant blue gem, so ancient and detailed that it seemed to glow with a life of its own. The light seemed to pulse from it, almost as if it were alive.

The gem pulsed once, a strange, rhythmic glow that felt alive, like it was drawing in the very energy of the room.

Iniyan's breath caught in his throat as he gazed at the gleaming blue gem. The markings on the stone were faint, but there, carved into the surface, were the words: "King

Draegor." The realization hit him like a cold wave.

The White King—the statue, the game, it all made sense now. This was no ordinary figure. This was King Draegor, the ruler of the lost kingdom of Zyphora. A king whose soul had been cursed, trapped in this game forever by the dark magic of Vraxen.

He had thought it was a mere statue, a relic of forgotten times, but now he understood. The curse that had bound Draegor's soul to this game was alive, pulsing with every beat of the gem. It was the very heart of the game. And now, Iniyan was part of it.

Ammama's words echoed in his mind once more: "Beware the game, Iniyan. For once you are pulled in, there is no escape." The weight of her warning settled heavily on his chest as he realized the depth of the danger surrounding him.

And then it clicked. The movement. The chess pieces moving in sync with the gem's pulse.

Every time the gem pulsed, the pieces shifted. The pawns marched forward. The rooks moved toward the center. The knights followed their own path, like clockwork. They weren't just moving randomly—they were following a sequence, a pattern. And the source of it all—the force that made them move—was this gem.

He stepped back, instinctively trying to distance himself from the gem, as if it were something that could pull him in. His mind raced. He had to get away from here, but how?

Every step he took felt like it was being watched. It wasn't just the chess pieces—something about the air felt wrong, as if the room itself was alive, watching, waiting.

He turned his back to the King statue, pressing his body against the cool marble. He closed his eyes for a moment, trying to steady his breath. He couldn't afford to panic. Not now. He had to think.

And then the voice came.

"You cannot hide from the game. The King sees all."

The voice was deep and cold, like it was coming from one of the pieces in the room. His spine stiffened as the realization hit him: the King wasn't just a statue. It was watching him. And if the King saw him, he would be done.

A chill swept through the room as the chess pieces began to move again—this time, with a purpose. But it wasn't just them. He could feel the force of the King's gaze, even though he couldn't see it. It was as if the statue's gem were pulling on his very soul, guiding the pieces, and locking him into the game.

The ground trembled again.

Iniyan's mind raced as he crouched behind the massive statue of the White King. He had realized it—it was the gem. The blue stone in the King's crown was the key to everything. The movements of the chess pieces, the strange energy in the room, it all made sense now. The pieces were responding to the gem's pulse, the silent command from the King.

But Iniyan wasn't about to sit back and let the game unfold without him. He needed control. He needed that gem.

The weight of the room was unbearable, as if the walls themselves were closing in.

"I have to do it," he whispered to himself, his voice shaking. "I have no choice."

With his heart pounding, he took a deep breath and moved toward the King's statue, his feet heavy on the marble floor. Every step felt like it was leading him into a trap. But he couldn't back down now.

The White King stood tall and proud, the blue gem gleaming in the soft light. As Iniyan reached up to touch it, his hand hesitated for just a second, as if the gem was daring him to take it. The whole room seemed to be holding its breath.

Just take it, he thought. Take it and make the pieces obey you.

Iniyan clung to the cold, smooth marble of the White King's statue, his fingers searching desperately for cracks or edges to hold on to. Each pull upward burned through his muscles, but he didn't stop. Below, the chess pieces watched with glowing eyes, their stony silence weighing on him. The air grew heavier the higher he climbed, as if the room itself resisted him. A sudden rumble shook the statue, and a massive rook crashed into its base, the impact sending a tremor through his grip. Iniyan's heart pounded, but he gritted his teeth and pushed forward, his focus locked on the glowing blue gem near the crown.

When he finally reached the top, he paused, breathless, his chest heaving. The gem pulsed with an eerie, rhythmic glow, its light growing stronger as he neared. Balancing precariously on the smooth surface, Iniyan stretched out a trembling hand. His grip faltered under the weight of his own body, but he steadied himself, clinging tightly to the crown's edge. With a deep breath, he reached again, the gem's light reflecting in his determined eyes.

His fingertips brushed the gem. The instant they made contact, a powerful jolt surged through him, like a shock of electricity. The gem's glow intensified, almost blinding him, and he had to squeeze his eyes shut for a moment to block out the light. His grip on the crown tightened as he adjusted his position, his legs swinging precariously as he tried to stabilize himself.

Iniyan opened his eyes and reached again, wrapping his fingers firmly around the gem. It was cold to the touch, smooth and unyielding, like it didn't want to be taken. He pulled hard, his muscles straining with the effort, but it didn't move. The gem remained firmly embedded in the crown.

Below him, the chess pieces started to shift. The pawns moved in unison, their heavy stone feet grinding against the floor. A knight reared up, its hooves crashing down with a loud, echoing thud that sent vibrations through the entire room. Another rook slid closer, its shadow looming over the base of the statue, making Iniyan's pulse quicken.

He didn't have much time.

Planting his feet against the marble for leverage, Iniyan gripped the gem with both hands and pulled with everything he had. The crown groaned in protest, tiny cracks forming around the gem's setting. His hands slipped against the smooth surface, but he adjusted his grip, ignoring the burning in his shoulders and the trembling in his legs. He gritted his teeth and pulled again, harder this time, the strain of it making his whole body ache.

With one final, desperate effort, the gem finally was free.

For a split second, nothing happened.

Then, all at once, there was a blinding flash. The light was so intense, Iniyan couldn't even keep his eyes open. It felt as though the gem had exploded with energy, pulling him into something far beyond his control.

I can't see, he thought, squeezing his eyes shut. Why can't I see?

As the light began to fade, a voice called to him—a voice that made his heart freeze.

"Iniyan..."

It was faint but unmistakable. Shifali. His heart skipped a beat.

"Iniyan..."

He opened his eyes, and the air around him felt different. Heavy, thick with an unfamiliar energy. The room of statues was gone. Instead, he stood on a massive chessboard. The black and white squares stretched endlessly in all directions, their stark patterns glowing faintly.

As his hand instinctively reached up, he froze. Resting on his head was a crown, cold and intricate. At its center, the blue gemstone pulsed faintly, its light casting a soft glow. The weight of the crown pressed down on him—not just physically, but with the realization that he was now wearing the symbol of the White King.

He wasn't just playing the game anymore. He was the White King.

His gaze locked onto someone across the board. It was Shifali. She was standing there, looking around in confusion, her eyes wide as she took in the vast chessboard and the strange, glowing pieces. She seemed unharmed but uncertain, her posture stiff as if unsure what was happening. Their eyes met for a moment, and Iniyan saw her lips move, mouthing his name, but the sound didn't reach him.

Before Iniyan could call out to her, movement drew his attention. The black pieces, shrouded in darkness moments ago, began to emerge. Towering pawns, rooks, and knights moved across the board with deliberate precision, their glowing eyes locking onto him. Their presence was menacing, and their slow, calculated movements sent a chill down his spine.

Then, from the far end of the board, a figure stepped forward—a towering figure clad in obsidian armor. The Black King. His crown glimmered with a dark, pulsing green gem, casting an eerie light across the board. His presence was suffocating, his gaze piercing as he surveyed the scene.

"Welcome to the game," the Black King said, his deep, growling voice reverberating through the space like a distant storm.

Shifali's head whipped around at the sound of his voice. Her confusion deepened as her eyes darted across the chessboard. The massive black pieces loomed ominously, their positions precise and deliberate. Then, her gaze fell on Iniyan.

At first, she noticed his wide-eyed expression, his stance frozen with the weight of the unfolding scene. But then her eyes traveled upward—to the crown on his head. The intricate metalwork, the faint glow of the bluc gem at its center—it all clicked. Her breath caught as realization struck her.

"Iniyan…" she whispered, her voice barely audible, though the name lingered in her thoughts.

The crown. The blue gemstone. The position he stood in. He wasn't just caught in the game—he was the White King.

Understanding dawned on her fully now. They weren't just in a strange place. They were in a battle—a living chess game—and Iniyan was its central figure, a piece thrust into the most dangerous position on the board.

"Who are you?" Iniyan demanded, his voice trembling but firm.

The Black King tilted his head, his lips curling into a cruel smile. Then, he laughed—a deep, guttural sound that echoed across the board. The laugh was mocking, filled with an arrogance that made Iniyan's skin crawl.

"Who am I?" the Black King repeated, his voice deep and commanding, as though the very air around them obeyed him. "I am the creator of this game, its ruler, and its master. The one who traps the foolish and the curious. I am the reason this game lives and breathes."

He stepped closer, his green gem casting a sinister glow across his armor. "You may call me....... **Vraxen**. I m the one who made this game. The architect of every soul bound to it. And now, you are part of my masterpiece."

Iniyan's breath hitched as the weight of the Black King's words sank in.

This wasn't just a game. It was a trap, a twisted creation of the sorcerer standing before him. And now, he and Shifali were caught in it.

The Black King's smile widened as he gestured to the chessboard. The black pieces shifted again, moving into their positions with precision, and the white pieces followed, as if compelled by an unseen force. The game board came to life, the pieces towering over them, radiating menace.

The game was on.

The Black King turned his piercing gaze to Iniyan, his voice low and cruel.

"Make your first move."

CHAPTER TWENTY-ONE

The Game Unfolds

Iniyan's fingers hovered over the white pawn in front of him. This first move felt too important, like it held the weight of everything to come. He wasn't just moving a piece—he was stepping into a world he barely understood.

"White Pawn to e4," he said, his voice steady.

The White Pawn advanced boldly, its small figure standing firm as if ready to face any threat. Across the board, the Black King gave a faint, almost mocking smile.

"Black Pawn to e5," the Black King said smoothly.

The Black Pawn slid forward to meet its counterpart. The battlefield was set; the center of the board now held the weight of both their intentions.

Iniyan's gaze shifted to his next move. "White Knight to f3."

The White Knight sprang into action, its lance appearing in a flash of light. It landed on f3 with precision, its gleaming weapon pointed toward the enemy line.

The Black King chuckled. "Black Knight to c6."

The Black Knight galloped into position, its spear angled defensively. The two Knights locked their gazes as though daring each other to make the first strike.

"White Bishop to b5," Iniyan commanded.

The White Bishop slid gracefully into position, its curved blade glinting in the dim light. Its focus was sharp, targeting the Black Knight. The Black King responded with ease.

"Black Pawn to a6."

The Black Pawn charged forward, challenging the White Bishop with its advance. Iniyan saw the danger and immediately withdrew his Bishop.
"White Bishop to a4," Iniyan said.

The White Bishop, its curved blade glinting in the dim light, gracefully retreated, maintaining its threat on the center of the board. Across the battlefield, the Black Knight stepped forward.

"Black Knight to f6," the Black King announced.

The Black Knight advanced, its lance steady, bolstering the defenses around its King. Both sides were maneuvering carefully, testing each other's resolve.

Iniyan's eyes flicked toward his King. It was time for a strategic repositioning. **"White King castling"**- he commanded.

The White King moved swiftly behind a protective wall of Pawns, the Rook taking its place on the e-file. It was a defensive move, but one that also prepared for the battles ahead.

The Black King nodded approvingly. "Black Bishop to e7."

The Black Bishop slid into position, its blade poised, ready to defend key squares around its King.

Iniyan's focus shifted. The time for defense was over. "White Rook to e1," he called.

The Rook, with its sheer weight and potential to crush its enemies, adjusted on the e-file, aligning its power toward the heart of the Black King's domain.

The Black King smirked. "Black Pawn to b5."

The Black Pawn surged forward, challenging the White Bishop. Iniyan saw the danger and immediately called his Bishop back.

"White Bishop to b3."

The Bishop retreated, its blade still sharp, maintaining its influence over the board's diagonal. The Black King responded with a calculated move.

"Black Pawn to d6."

The Black Pawn moved to d6, fortifying the center and providing a robust defense for the King. Iniyan countered with a strengthening move of his own.

"White Pawn to c3."

The White Pawn stepped up, supporting the center and preparing for future advances. The Black King took a moment, then made his next move.

"Black King castling."

The Black King followed suit, positioning himself behind a secure fortress of pieces. Both sides were now fully prepared for an intense battle.

Iniyan's attention turned to the safety of his Bishop. "White Pawn to h3."

The Pawn moved to h3, creating a sanctuary for the Bishop and discouraging any potential threats from the Black side.

The Black King didn't wait. "Black Knight to a5."

The Black Knight leaped forward, its lance gleaming ominously, setting its sights on the White Bishop stationed at b3. The pressure on the board increased, each piece carefully poised for the inevitable clashes ahead.

"White Bishop to c2," Iniyan declared.

The Bishop slid back, its blade still poised to strike. The Black King pressed the advantage.

"Black Pawn to c5."

The Black Pawn lunged forward staking its claim on the center.

"White Pawn to d4."

The Pawn at d4 advanced, opening lines for the White pieces to attack. The Black Queen moved forward, her sword glowing faintly.

"Black Queen to c7."

The Queen took her place, her presence commanding and foreboding. Iniyan's heart quickened as he saw the battlefield shifting.

"White Pawn captures on e5," he called out.

The White Pawn surged forward, fists clenched, and delivered a powerful punch to the Black Pawn guarding e5.

The Black Pawn staggered but retaliated with a fierce uppercut, their blows echoing like thunder. After a brutal exchange, the **Black Pawn landed a decisive strike**, sending the White Pawn crumbling into the glowing board before reclaiming its place at e5, standing victorious yet vigilant.

Both slammed into the square with a force that shook the board, sending tremors through the ground. Shifali stepped back instinctively, her eyes widening.

"Iniyan," she whispered.

Iniyan's heart raced. He could feel it now—the air was alive, charged with something dark and ancient. Every move wasn't just strategy—*it was war*. The realization struck him deeply. Iniyan wasted no time.

"White Knight to d2."

The White Knight joined the fray, its lance poised to strike at key positions. The Black King smirked and advanced.

"Black Pawn to c4."

The Pawn moved aggressively, disrupting the White formation. Iniyan countered with precision.

"White Knight to f1."

The Knight shifted to f1, positioning itself for a strategic assault. The Black Bishop moved into play.

"Black Bishop to e6."

The Bishop slid diagonally, its curved blade gleaming menacingly as it targeted the vulnerable squares near the White King. Iniyan saw an opportunity.

"White Knight to e3."

The Knight leaped forward, taking control of the board's center. The Black King's forces responded.

"Black Rook to d8."

The Rook rumbled into position, its sheer weight a threat to anything in its path. Iniyan adjusted his strategy.

"White Queen to e2."

The Queen advanced, her glowing sword radiating authority as she coordinated with the other pieces. The Black Knight leaped forward.

"Black Knight to h5."

The Black Knight's presence was menacing, its spear aimed at the White King's defenses. Iniyan called his next move.

"White Knight to f5."

The Knight sprang into action, targeting the Black Bishop with precision. The Black King retaliated without hesitation.

"**Black Bishop captures on f5.**"

The Black Bishop lunged forward, its curved blade gleaming as it struck the White Knight with a decisive blow. The Knight staggered before collapsing, its lance clattering to the board and vanishing into the glowing squares.

"**White Pawn recaptures on f5**."

Without hesitation, the White Pawn stepped up, its fists glowing with energy. With a forceful punch, it drove the Bishop back, reclaiming the square. The Black Knight, sensing the shift in momentum, cautiously retreated, its spear still poised for defense.

The board was alive with tension, every move calculated, every piece poised for battle. Both sides were locked in a desperate struggle for dominance. Iniyan and Shifali exchanged a glance—they knew this battle was far from over, but they were ready to fight for every square.

Now it was clear: each piece wielded its own weapon in battle.

- **Pawns** fought with their fists, relying on raw determination.
- **Knights** wielded lances, striking swiftly and precisely.
- **Bishops** carried elegant curved blades, deadly in their precision.
- **Rooks** relied on their sheer weight, crushing everything in their path.
- **Queens** were armed with glowing swords, commanding the board with deadly grace.
- **The Kings**, though yet to act, radiated an ominous power.

Iniyan and Shifali stood firm. They weren't just playing for survival anymore. Every move counted. Every piece mattered. Together, they were determined to fight—and win.

CHAPTER TWENTY-TWO

TURNING POINT

Iniyan's mind was racing. The game had come down to this—a few pieces left, each move more critical than the last. On the board, the White side was down to two pawns, a Queen, a Rook, and the King. The Black side was similarly weakened, with only a Queen, King, and Bishop remaining. The entire board had transformed into a battlefield—each piece symbolizing a player's last hope, each move a desperate grasp at survival.

The board was a battlefield, with Iniyan and Shifali standing on the edge of their seats, knowing every decision could change their fate.

Shifali's voice broke the tense silence. "Iniyan, we need to give the Black King a check."

Iniyan turned to her, his face pale with doubt. "Are you sure? You've seen how this game works, Shifali. Every piece uses weapons. If the Black Queen strikes back, it could—" He hesitated, swallowing hard. "It could kill you."

Shifali's eyes burned with determination. "We don't have another choice. If we don't act now, he'll corner us. This is the only way to force a mistake."

Iniyan shook his head, his fists clenched. "But what if—"

"Iniyan," Shifali interrupted, her tone firm yet understanding. "You know the plan. Trust me. We can't hesitate now."

His heart pounded as he struggled with the decision. Every instinct screamed at him to protect her, to stop this madness. But deep down, he knew she was right. They couldn't afford to waste a move.

Finally, with visible reluctance, he nodded. "Fine. But... be careful."

Shifali gave him a reassuring smile before stepping forward. Her White Queen glided across the board with an air of authority, her glowing sword appearing in her hand as she reached her target.

"White Queen to e7," Shifali declared.

White Queen to e7—Check.

The Black King's green gem flared ominously as he faced the threat. He laughed coldly, his voice echoing across the board. "You think a simple check can stop me? Black Queen to e7."

The Black Queen surged forward, her dark sword gleaming in her hand. Sparks flew as her weapon clashed with the White Queen's blade. Shifali, the White Queen held her ground, but the Black Queen pressed on, her strikes swift and relentless.

Iniyan's breath caught in his throat as he watched the battle. His hands tightened into fists, every muscle in his body screaming to intervene, but he knew he couldn't.

The Black Queen's blade swung in a wide arc, knocking the White Queen back. With a final, ruthless strike, the White Queen fell. Shifali, the White Queen was out, dissolving into the glowing board. The loss of her connection to the Queen hit her like a blow.

"No," Iniyan whispered, his voice filled with anguish. His worst fear had come true.

The Black King's laughter rumbled across the board. "You sacrificed your Queen for nothing. Your plan has failed, and now you'll watch as I dismantle your army."

"Now, Iniyan," he imagined her saying, her voice unwavering despite the pain. "The next move."

Iniyan's hesitation melted away as he saw the opportunity before him. The Black Queen, focused entirely on her attack, had left herself vulnerable. Iniyan called out the move with renewed determination.

"White Rook to e7."

The White Rook rumbled forward, its massive frame and crushing force bearing down on the Black Queen. With a single, devastating blow, the Rook struck the Black Queen, sending her sprawling. Her sword clattered to the ground as her figure dissolved into the board.

The Black King stared at the board in stunned silence. The loss of his Queen had completely shifted the balance of the game. He hadn't expected to lose so much so quickly.

Iniyan knew they were close. But the Black King, ever the strategist, wasn't giving up just yet.

"You think you've won?" the Black King said, his voice dark and cold. "It's not over yet. This game could end in a draw, and even then, you cannot escape it."

The threat hung in the air like a dark cloud. Even if it ended in a draw, Iniyan and Shifali would remain trapped in this cursed game forever.

CHAPTER TWENTY-THREE

THE FINAL MOVE

Iniyan knew that this was his moment. There was only one path forward now. His heart pounded in his chest, but he remained calm, focusing only on the pawn in front of him.

With a sharp breath, he moved his White Pawn forward, pushing it from d7 to d8. The moment it crossed the finish line, it transformed.

White Pawn to d8—Promotion.

"Checkmate."

The voice echoed, but it wasn't just a voice in his head—it was the voice of the game itself. The transformation was complete.

A new White Queen emerged from the ranks of pawns. But it wasn't just any Queen—it was Shifali.

As the pawn turned into the White Queen, Shifali's figure shimmered and shifted. She took her position on the square, her eyes locking with Iniyan's. There was no need for words. She knew what had to be done.

And then, something miraculous happened.

The Black King's face turned pale with shock as he saw the White Queen approach him. He had no moves left. The game had been won, but in a way he hadn't anticipated.

His grip on the game—the hold that had been so unshakable—was slipping, and he didn't even realize it.

"**Checkmate,**" the voice whispered again, its presence now stronger, almost taunting. The Black King still didn't move.

Shifali stepped forward with a calm grace. The Black King's eyes flickered to the gem on his head—the green stone that had once seemed so powerful. It was the source of his control over the game. But now, it was the last obstacle to their escape.

As she drew closer, the tension in the air became suffocating. Shifali could feel the power radiating from the gem, its dark energy clawing at her as if trying to keep her away. She hesitated for a brief moment, her fingers trembling, but then she clenched her fists and steeled herself.

"**Weapon of mine, come to me!**" she commanded, her voice resonating with an otherworldly authority. It was as if the battlefield itself answered her call.

A blinding light enveloped her, and from it emerged a sword unlike any other. Its blade was glowing with an ethereal brilliance, pulsating with raw energy. It felt alive in her hands, its presence almost demonic, a force that mirrored the darkness of the Black King but burned with the fire of justice.

The Black King's composure faltered for the first time. "You dare?" he snarled, his voice trembling with both fury and fear.

Shifali didn't reply. Her gaze was fixed on the gem. With a swift leap, she closed the distance between them, her movements fluid and unyielding. The Black King raised his hands as if to block her, but the game's rules bound him—he couldn't defend himself now.

The air grew heavy as Shifali swung the sword, its light cutting through the darkness like a beacon. The blade struck the gem, sending a shockwave across the board. The gem resisted, its dark energy lashing out at her, wrapping around her like fiery chains. She screamed as the searing pain coursed through her, her vision blurring.

But she didn't stop. With her free hand, she gripped the gem tightly, its surface cold and slick, pulsating with malevolence. She could feel it fighting back, trying to break her resolve, but she refused to let go.

Summoning every ounce of strength within her, Shifali raised the sword one final time. Her voice rang out, filled with defiance. **"This ends now!"**

The sword came down, striking the gem with a deafening crack. The impact unleashed an explosion of light and sound, blinding everyone on the board. The green gem shattered into a thousand pieces, its fragments dissolving into the air like smoke.

The Black King let out a guttural roar, his form flickering and crumbling like ash in the wind. The game's hold over the board broke instantly. The pieces froze mid-movement, their menacing presence fading as they turned into lifeless stone.

The moment the gem came off, the entire board shuddered. The pieces that had once been so menacing seemed to lose their power. The Black King's sinister smile disappeared, his green gem now nothing but an ordinary stone. The game had ended. The curse was broken.

The air in the room was thick with tension. The giant marble statue, once standing tall, now began to tremble, cracks spidering up its surface like the first signs of a storm. Iniyan's heart raced. There was no time. They had done everything they could, but now... the final blow was coming.

The room seemed to hold its breath as the other statues shook violently.

Crack!

The sound echoed like thunder, and the air was filled with dust and shattered stone. Iniyan's eyes widened in horror as the statues began to crumble. His mind screamed out in panic, but it was too late.

The scene around him suddenly went silent. Time seemed to slow.

In that brief, almost surreal moment, everything was muted. The room fell into stillness. A few fragments of the crumbling statue flew through the air.

One of the pieces, a sharp chunk of stone, flew towards Shifali.

Her eyes widen as she instinctively ducks, but it's too fast. The stone hits her forehead with a sickening crack.

Her body lurches back, her body beginning to fall. Iniyan reaches out, his arm stretching towards her, his heart pounding in his chest.

No!

Her body seems to fall forever, her movements almost graceful despite the danger. Her eyes flutter as the world spins around her. Then, just as her head inches closer to the cold, hard ground, a hand shoots out and catches her.

As she fell, Iniyan rushed forward, desperate to reach her. Just before her head hit the cold floor, a hand shot out, catching her.

Her fall is halted.

She is gently cradled in someone's arms. The hand that holds her is warm, strong—comforting. Slowly, she is laid down, her head resting against something soft, something familiar.

The world is blurry at first, everything spinning. Then, as her vision clears, she sees the face of the person holding her.

It's him.

INIYAN.

Tears fill his eyes, his gaze full of raw emotion. His lips tremble as he looks at her, his hand gently cupping her face. The softness in his eyes is undeniable, filled with relief and pain.

Shifali's breath catches, her heart racing. Her hand instinctively reaches up to touch his face.

"I... I thought I lost you," Iniyan whispers, his voice thick with emotion.

"I'm right here," Shifali says softly, her voice weak but reassuring. She manages a faint smile, her hand brushing against his cheek. "I'm... not going anywhere."

They look at each other, a perfect stillness in the chaos of everything around them. It's as if, in that moment, nothing else matters—only the connection between them.

Just a few feet away, glinting in the dim light, lies something that could change everything.

The gem.

The green stone that had once been the source of the Black King's power, now lying broken on the floor like an insignificant trinket.

For a moment, the world seemed to fade away, and the two of them just looked at each other. Iniyan's heart swelled with relief and love, while Shifali's gaze was filled with tenderness and understanding.

Iniyan then placed a hand on her shoulder, a gentle pat that spoke volumes. It was a silent acknowledgment of everything she had done, a gesture filled with gratitude and admiration.

Shifali gave a small nod, her lips curving into a faint, tired smile. No words were needed. The battle was over.The battle was over. The game was finished. And they were free.

CHAPTER TWENTY-FOUR

The Crown's Awakening

The mysterious room was silent, save for the faint sound of the clock's ticking in the distance. The air, thick with tension moments before, now seemed to breathe with a strange calm. The Black King, whose presence had once commanded the space, now lay motionless on the chessboard, his power dissipating into the empty air.

The light from above flickered, casting a soft, dim glow across the chessboard. It was as if the room itself had exhaled, and the weight of the darkness that had suffocated it for so long began to lift. The White King and Queen, once overshadowed by the dark pieces, now stood at the center of the room, bathed in the gentle beam of light that seemed to recognize their victory.

The White Queen stood tall and strong, her posture steady and confident. The shadows that had once surrounded her seemed to pull back, as if they were acknowledging her new power. Her presence, no longer hidden in the dark, filled the room with a quiet energy. The White King, too, regained his strength. Once bent and broken, he now stood firmly beside her. Together, they made a strong pair, bringing a sense of balance and calm to the chessboard.

The dim light above them grew brighter, casting long shadows across the black pieces. The darkness that had once filled the room began to fade, replaced by a soft, glowing light. The Black pieces, which had once seemed powerful and threatening, now appeared small and insignificant compared to the strength that radiated from the White King and Queen.

As the light from above grew stronger, something unexpected happened. A soft glow appeared on the heads of the White King and Queen. It was a blue gem, bright and shimmering, as if it had always been there but had just revealed itself. The gems sparkled, adding an extra layer of power to their already commanding presence.

The room, now filled with light and peace, seemed to acknowledge the transformation. The White King and Queen, with their blue gems glowing, stood as symbols of victory and strength. The dark pieces were now nothing more than shadows in the background, their power completely gone. The game was over, and with the shining blue gems, the White King and Queen were finally at the peak of their power, their victory complete.